The ultimate kings of seduction!

THE PLAYBOYS
AND HEROES
COLLECTION

Th   layboys and Heroes large print collection
gives you lavish stories of luxury
from your favourite top authors
in easier-to-read print.

PASSION: THE DESERT SHEIKH'S CAPTIVE WIFE

Lynne Graham

First published in Great Britain 2007
by Mills & Boon, an imprint of Harlequin (UK) Limited,
Large Print edition 2012
Harlequin (UK) Limited,
Eton House, 18-24 Paradise Road, Richmond, Surrey TW9 1SR

© Lynne Graham 2007

ISBN: 978 0 263 23054 3

Harlequin (UK) policy is to use papers that are natural, renewable and recyclable products and made from wood grown in sustainable forests. The logging and manufacturing process conform to the legal environmental regulations of the country of origin.

Printed and bound in Great Britain
by CPI Antony Rowe, Chippenham, Wiltshire

Lynne Graham was born in Northern Ireland, and has been a keen Mills & Boon® reader since her teens. She is very happily married, with an understanding husband who has learned to cook since she started to write! Her five children keep her on her toes. She has a very large dog, which knocks everything over, a very small terrier, which barks a lot, and two cats. When time allows, Lynne is a keen gardener.

CHAPTER ONE

'HAVE I met anyone whom I would like to marry?' Rashad, Crown Prince of Bakhar almost laughed out loud as he considered his father's gently voiced question. Engrained good manners, however, restrained such a blunt response. 'No, I fear not.'

King Hazar surveyed his son and heir with concealed disquiet. His guilty conscience was pricked by the truth that he had been blessed by Rashad's birth, for his son was everything a future monarch should be. His sterling qualities had shone like a beacon during those dark days when Bakhar had suffered under the despotic rule of Sadiq, Hazar's uncle. In the eyes of the people, Rashad could do no wrong; he had endured many cruelties, but had still emerged a hero from the war that had restored the legitimate line to the throne. Even the rumours that the Crown Prince was regarded as a notorious womaniser abroad barely raised a brow, since it was accepted that he had earned the right to enjoy his liberty.

'There comes a time when a man must settle down,' King Hazar remarked with all the awkwardness of one who had never been anything other than settled in his habits. 'And put aside more worldly pursuits.'

His lean and darkly handsome features grim, Rashad stared stonily out at the exquisite gardens that were his father's pride and joy. Maybe when he was older he too would get a thrill out of pruning topiary, he reflected wryly. Although he had a great affection for the older man, father and son were not close. How could they have been? Rashad had been only four years old when he'd been torn from his mother's arms and denied all further contact with his parents. In the following two decades, he had learned to trust nobody and keep his own counsel. By the time he had been reunited with his family, he had been an adult, a survivor and a battle-hardened soldier, trained to put duty and discipline above all other virtues. But on this particular issue he was not prepared to meet his father's expectations.

'I don't want to get married,' Rashad declared levelly.

King Hazar was unprepared for that bold response, which offered neither apology nor the possibility of compromise. Assuming that he had broached the subject clumsily, he said earnestly, 'I believe that marriage will greatly add to your happiness.'

Rashad almost winced at that simplistic assurance. He had no such expectation. Only once had a woman made Rashad happy, but almost as quickly he had discovered that he was living in a fool's paradise. He had never forgotten the lesson. He liked his freedom and he liked sex. In short he enjoyed women, but there was only one space for a woman to fill in his private life and that was in his bed. And just as, when it came to food, he preferred a varied diet, he had no desire to have any woman foisted on him on a permanent basis. 'I'm afraid I cannot agree with you on that issue.'

The older man ignored the decided chill that laced the atmosphere and suppressed a sigh. He wished that he'd had the opportunity to acquire just a smidgeon of his son's superior education and sophistication so that they might talk on more equal terms. Most of all he longed for the ability to deal with the son he loved with a wholly clear conscience, but unhappily that was not possible. 'I have never known us to be at odds. I must have expressed my hopes badly. Or perhaps I took you too much by surprise.'

Rashad folded his wide sensual mouth. 'Nothing you could say will change my mind. I have no desire for a wife.'

'Rashad…' His royal father was aghast at the stubborn inflexibility of that refusal, for his son was not known for his changeability. 'You are so popular with our people that I believe you could marry any woman you chose. Perhaps you are concerned about the type of woman you might be expected to marry. It is my belief that even a foreigner would be acceptable.'

Brilliant dark eyes veiled and grim, Rashad had fallen very still at that reference to the possibility of a foreign bride. He wondered if the older man was recalling his son's disastrous infatuation with an Englishwoman five years ago. The very suspicion of that stung Rashad's ferocious pride. He and his father had buried the ill-fated episode without ever discussing it.

'We live in a modern world. Yet you believe that I must behave exactly as you and my forefathers behaved and marry young to produce a son and heir,' Rashad delivered with cool, crisp diction. 'I do not believe that such sacrifice is necessary. I have three older sisters with a string of healthy sons between them. In the future, one of those boys might stand as my heir.'

'But none of them have a royal father. One day, you will be king. Will you disappoint our people? What have you got against marriage?'

the older man demanded in bewilderment. 'You have so much to offer.'

Everything but a heart and faith in woman-kind, Rashad affixed with inward impatience. 'I have nothing against the institution of marriage. It was right for you but it would not be right for me.'

'At least reflect on what I have said,' King Hazar urged. 'We will talk about this again.'

Having defended his right to freedom as reso-lutely as he had once fought for the freedom of the Bakhari people from a repressive regime, Rashad strode out through the vast ante-room beyond his father's private quarters. It was thronged with senior ministers and courtiers, who bowed very low as he passed. One after another, guards presented arms and saluted as Rashad progressed through the ancient court-yards and corridors to his suite of offices.

'Oh…I meant to surprise you, Your Royal Highness.' A very attractive brunette with almond-shaped brown eyes and creamy skin, set off by a sleek coil of dark brown hair, straightened from the refreshments she had been setting out in the spacious outer office. In acknowledgement of his arrival, she bent low as did the staff, who had been engaged in answering the phones. 'We all know that you often work so hard that you forget to eat.'

Although Rashad would have preferred privacy at that moment, the courteous formalities expected of a prince were second nature to him. Farah was a distant relation. With modest smiles and light conversation, Rashad was served with mint tea and tiny cakes. Evidently word of his father's hope of marrying him off was out in the élite court circle of Bakhar, so Rashad did not make the mistake of sitting down and prolonging the exchange of pleasantries. He knew that the whole exercise was designed to impress him as to Farah's suitability as a royal bride and hostess.

'I couldn't help noticing your alumni magazine, Your Royal Highness,' Farah remarked. 'You must be proud of having attained a first from Oxford University.'

His level dark deep set eyes shadowed. 'Indeed,' he said flatly, and dismissed her with a polite nod. 'You must excuse me. I have an appointment.'

Having swept up the magazine she had drawn to his attention, Rashad entered his palatial office. He wondered how many previous issues he had ignored and left unread over the years. He had few fond memories of his time as a student in England. In defiance of that thought he leafed through the publication, only to fall still when the fleeting glimpse of a woman's face suddenly focused his attention on one page and a photograph in particular. It was Matilda Crawford arriving at an academic function, her hand resting on the arm of a distinguished older man in a dinner jacket.

Rashad spread the magazine open on his desk with lean brown hands that were not quite steady. It was pure primitive rage, not nerves, that powered him. Matilda's pale blond hair was pulled back from her face, and she was wearing a rather prim high-necked brown dress. But then, her natural beauty required no adornment:

she had the fair hair, ivory skin and turquoise-blue eyes of a true English rose. His perfect white teeth gritted as he studied the caption below the photo. She was not named but her partner was: Professor Evan Jerrold, the philanthropist. A rich man—of course a rich man! No doubt another gullible sucker ripe for the plucking, Rashad thought with fierce bitterness and distaste.

He was exasperated that he was still sensitive to the sight of Tilda and the regrettable memories she roused. It had been, however, an unsavoury incident in his life and a reminder that he had human flaws. Five years earlier, Rashad might have been seasoned on the battlefield and idolised by his countrymen as a saviour, but his great-uncle Sadiq had succeeded in keeping him a virtual prisoner in Bakhar. Rashad had lived under constant threat and surveillance. He had been twenty-five years old by the time his father had been restored to the throne and he himself had been eager to take advantage of the freedom that had been denied him.

It had been King Hazar who suggested that Rashad complete his academic studies in England. Rashad might have inherited his mother's intellectual brilliance and his father's shrewdness but, in those days, he had had little experience of the ways of Western females. Within days of his arrival in Oxford, he had become infatuated with an outrageously unsuitable young woman.

Tilda Crawford had been a bar-girl, a one-time exotic dancer and a deceitful gold-digging slut. But she had told Rashad poignant stories about her bullying stepfather and her family's sufferings at his hands. She had judged her audience well, Rashad acknowledged with derision. Brought up to believe that it was his duty to help those weaker than himself, he had flipped straight into gallant rescue mode. Duped by her beauty and her lies, he had come dangerously close to asking her to marry him. What a future queen that lowborn Jezebel would have made! The acid bite of the humiliation that had been inflicted on him still had the power to sting Rashad's ego afresh.

He squared his broad shoulders and lifted his proud dark head high. It really was time to draw a line beneath the sleazy episode and consign his regrets to the past. Only now could he see that this feat could scarcely be achieved while the wrongdoers went unpunished. Without a doubt, the requirements of truth and decency had not been served by the dignified silence he had maintained. Indeed, had he not inadvertently made it easier for Tilda Crawford to go on to defraud other wealthy men? He might well save her elderly admirer from a similar trial, he thought with bleak satisfaction. Offenders should be called to account for their sins, not permitted to continue enjoying the fruits of their dishonesty.

Rashad studied the photo of Tilda again and marvelled at how much better he felt now that he had recognised where his ultimate duty lay. Action was required, not strategic withdrawal. He contacted his chief accountant to confirm that not a single payment had yet been received on the interest-free loan he had advanced to the Crawford family. He was not surprised to have his worst expectations fulfilled. He gave the order that the matter should be pursued with diligence. Powered by a strong sense of justice, he tossed the magazine aside.

Pushing the mass of her long blond hair back behind her ear, Tilda studied her mother, Beth, in total consternation and asked for a second time, 'How much do you owe?'

The tear-stained older woman gazed back at her daughter with wretched eyes and repeated the figure shakily. 'I'm sorry; I'm so sorry about this. I should've told you months ago but I couldn't face it. I've been hiding my head in the sand and hoping all the trouble would go away.'

Tilda was in serious shock at the amount of money her mother confessed to owing. It was simply huge. Surely there was some mistake or misunderstanding? She could not imagine how Beth could possibly have got into that much debt. Who would have loaned her perennially cash-strapped parent so much money? How on earth could anyone ever have believed that Beth might repay such a vast sum? She reminded herself that interest charges could be very steep and began to ask more pertinent questions in an effort to establish how and when such a debt had originated.

'When did you take out the loan?'

Beth wiped at her reddened eyes, but did not look directly at her daughter. 'Five years ago…but I'm not sure you could describe it as a loan.'

Tilda was astonished that her mother could have kept it a secret for so long. But she could remember very well how much of a struggle it had been back then just to put food on the table. She was simply bewildered by Beth's uncertainty about whether or not she had taken out a loan. 'Can I see the paperwork?'

The older woman scrambled up and went into the very depths of a cupboard from which she withdrew a plastic container. She shot her daughter a sheepish glance. 'I've had to hide the letters so that you and your brothers and sisters didn't see them and ask me what they were about.'

As a sizeable pile of letters was tipped out onto the table Tilda swallowed back a groan of disbelief. 'How long is it since you were last able to make a payment?'

Pushing her short fair hair off her brow in a nervous gesture, Beth sent Tilda an uneasy look. 'I've never made a payment—'

'Never?' Tilda interrupted in dismay.

'There wasn't the money at first and I thought that I would start making payments when things improved,' the small blonde woman confided, shredding a tissue between her trembling hands. 'But things never did improve enough. There was always a bill or someone needing new shoes or bus fares…or Christmas would come along and I hated disappointing the children. They would go without so much for the rest of the year.'

'I know.' Leafing through the heap of unopened letters, Tilda breathed out and in again very slowly and carefully. She knew she dared not show how appalled she was by what she was finding out. Her mother was a vulnerable woman, prone to panic attacks. She needed her daughter to be calm and supportive. It was, after all, over four years since Beth had last left the house to face an outside world that had become so threatening to her. Agoraphobia, a fear of open spaces, had made Beth's home her prison. But it had not stopped the older woman from working for her living. A whizz with a sewing machine, Beth had a regular clientele for whom she tailored clothes and made soft furnishings. Unfortunately, however, she did not earn very much.

'Exactly how did you get the loan?' Tilda prompted in confusion. 'Surely nobody came to the house to offer you that much money?'

Across the table Beth worried at her lower lip with her teeth and shifted uncomfortably. There was a shamefaced look on her face. 'This is the bit I really didn't want to tell you. In fact, it's why I felt I had to keep it all a secret. It made me feel so guilty and I didn't want to upset you. You see, I asked Rashad for the money and he gave it to me.'

Every scrap of colour ebbed from Tilda's oval face. With her flawless features stretched taut over

her delicate bone structure, her turquoise-blue
eyes seemed brighter than ever against her pallor.
'Rashad…' she repeated weakly, her heart sinking
like a stone and shame grabbing her by the throat.
'You actually asked *him* to help us out?'

'Don't look at me like that!' Beth gasped
strickenly, her unhappiness overflowing into
tears. 'Rashad once said that we all felt like part
of his family, and that that's how families always
work in Bakhar—everyone looking out for
everybody else. I was convinced he was going
to marry you. I thought it was all right to accept
his financial help.'

Tilda was aghast at an explanation that rang all
too true from a woman as naïve as her mother
was. When Rashad had visited her home he had
appeared to like her large and boisterous family.
In fact, it was only during those occasions that
she had ever seen Rashad fully relax his guard.
He had played rough-and-tumble games with
her brothers, taught one of her sisters mathe-
matical long division and read stories to the
youngest. Unsurprisingly, her mother had

become a huge admirer of his. Tilda had never had the heart to tell the older woman why and how she and Rashad had broken up. Pushing herself clumsily upright, Tilda walked over to the living-room window. A busy road lay beyond the front garden of the semi-detached house, but Tilda was so lost in a tide of angry, painful thoughts that she was not aware of the traffic.

While she was very loyal to her mother she was cringing at what she had just learned. She was shattered to learn a full five years after the event that her relationship with Rashad had begat a financial angle that she had known nothing about! Surely that must have had a negative effect on Rashad's view of her? She would have died a thousand deaths of shame had she known about that money at the time.

Rashad was fabulously wealthy and very generous. Had he simply taken pity on Beth? Or had he cherished a darker motive? Had he believed that money might make Tilda less nervous of surrendering her body to him? Had he intended it as the purchase price of her virginity? Her pride writhed at that sordid suspicion. Was she being hugely unfair to him? She thought that actions sometimes spoke louder than words. She had not slept with Rashad and he had ditched her without an ounce of compassion or decency.

'I was desperate,' Beth admitted in a stricken undertone. 'I knew it wasn't right but your stepfather had got us into such a mess with the mortgage payments. I was terrified that we were going to end up homeless.'

It took enormous effort but Tilda managed to close a mental door on the potent image of Prince Rashad Hussein Al-Zafar, with whom she'd had the poor taste to fall madly in love at the age of eighteen. That reference to her mother's ghastly second husband helped to distract her. Scott Morrison had married Beth when she was a widow with two young children. On the surface a glib and handsome charmer, he had been a terrible bully, who had systematically robbed his stepfamily of their financial security. The birth of three more children and the stress of dealing with an unfaithful and dishonest husband had led to Beth's panic attacks and her eventual diagnosis of agoraphobia.

'When I asked Rashad for help, he said that he would buy the house and keep it in his name so that Scott couldn't get his hands on it…'

Tilda whirled round, depth-charged by that information out of her recollections and back into the all-too-threatening present. On every front that admission came as a shock to Tilda. 'Are you telling me that Rashad also *owns* this house?' she gasped in horror.

'Yes. At first that made me feel that we were all safe and secure!' the older woman suddenly sobbed.

'Why don't you make a cup of tea while I take a look at some of these letters?' Tilda suggested, hoping that that routine task would help her mother to calm down. Yet her own self-discipline was being equally challenged by what she had discovered. Although she was determined not to give way to a growing sense of panic, she could not stop Rashad's name from rhyming and purring like a derisive echo at the back of her mind.

Eager to hide the fact that she was frantic with worry, Tilda sorted the mostly unopened letters into rough piles according to date. But flashes of memory kept on attacking her from all sides: Rashad, so breathtakingly handsome she hadn't been able to take her eyes off him the first time she saw him; Rashad, the last time she had seen him, kissing another woman. Having dumped her, he had moved on with breathtaking speed. Her mind was quick to back away from that final recollection and she began reading the letters. Silence fell while she speedily absorbed their contents. Unhappily what she learned from the exercise was not good news.

To begin with, Rashad, or more probably his representatives in the matter, had engaged a London legal firm while ensuring that Beth received advice from another solicitor. The purchase price of the house had been fair. A further substantial amount of money had been advanced to settle several outstanding debts.

Wincing as she totted up figures in her head, Tilda became more and more tense. If anything, her mother had underestimated the size of her debt. A contract that allowed for every eventuality had been signed. Her mother had been given a whole year to get her affairs in order before she was asked whether she wished to take out a mortgage to buy the house back or instead opt to pay rent as a tenant. Tilda came on a copy of the tenancy agreement that her mother had signed.

'What made you decide to sign a tenancy agreement?' Tilda queried dry-mouthed.

'The solicitor came to see me here and I had to make a choice about what I was going to do.'

'But you haven't paid any rent, have you?' her daughter prompted, having already seen a worrying missive that referred to rent arrears.

'No. I couldn't afford to.' Beth eyed the younger woman fearfully.

'Not even *one* payment?' Tilda thought that there should have been enough income to at least pay the rent but, as quickly, blamed herself for not having taken more of an interest in the family finances.

'No, not one.' Beth would not meet her daughter's troubled gaze, and Tilda wondered uneasily if there was something that she wasn't being told.

'Mum…are there any other problems?' Tilda pressed.

Beth gave her a frightened look and shook her head. 'Now that you've seen the letters, what do you think?'

Shelving the ESP that was giving her the suspicion there was something else amiss, Tilda knew she could not say what she thought about the letters. Her mother was a loving and caring parent, adored by every one of her five children. She was also extremely kind and hard-working, but when it came to dealing with money or problem husbands Beth was pretty much useless. By ignoring the letters, the older woman had acted as her own worst enemy. More recent missives had taken on the cold, clipped edge of threat. *They were facing eviction from their home.*

Tilda felt as if spooky fingers were tightening round her lungs, for the challenge of delivering such terrifying news to her mother was at that moment beyond her. Beth was too frightened even to walk down the drive to the front gate, so how could she possibly cope with the awful upheaval and disgrace of being literally cast out on the street? And if *she* could not cope, how would it affect Tilda's four younger siblings?

'Tilda...' Beth surveyed her daughter with a heavy heart '...I'm really sorry I didn't tell you about this months ago, but I felt so guilty about having married Scott. Everything that's gone wrong for us since then is my fault.'

'You can't blame yourself for marrying him. He didn't show his true colours until after the wedding and now he's out of our lives, so let's not go back there,' Tilda urged in a deliberately upbeat tone. 'Stop worrying about this. I'll look into it and see what I can sort out.'

The buzz of the doorbell sounded extraordinarily loudly in the strained silence.

Dismay tightening her features as she checked

her watch, Beth flew upright. 'That'll be a customer. I'd better splash my face with some cold water!'

'Go ahead. I'll answer the door.' Tilda was grateful for that timely interruption, for she did not want to be tempted into soothing her mother by offering empty assurances that everything would come all right. Even in the grip of shock as Tilda still was, she could see little prospect of a happy ending to her family's predicament. After all, only repayment of the debt could settle it and they were all as poor as church mice.

Frustration hurtled through Tilda, who felt as if her brain was suffering from a stress overload. Why, oh, why, had she given up a steady job to pursue an academic qualification for three years? But the decision *had* made sense at the time, offering as it did the prospect of a career with eventual excellent earning potential. Unfortunately it meant that now she had no savings and had a large student loan to pay back. Even though she was currently working full time again in a position with good prospects, she was a junior member of staff and her salary was not generous.

Tilda found her former employer, Evan Jerrold, on the doorstep. Once again Evan had his arms wrapped round a fat roll of curtain fabric. The sight would have provoked a smile from Tilda on a normal day, because in old-fashioned parlance—and he was an old-fashioned man— Evan was sweet on her mother. After a chance meeting with Beth one day when he had given Tilda a lift into work, the older man had gradually become a regular visitor. For months now he had been dreaming up new furnishing projects that gave him ample opportunity to ask Beth to advise him on colour, fabric and style.

Tilda showed Evan through to her mother's workroom at the back of the house. The kindly older man had originally encouraged Tilda to give up her office job and go to university. An academic, who had inherited a thriving family firm, Evan had ensured that Tilda always had a job there during her college vacations. Tilda went into the kitchen to gather up the letters and take them upstairs. She was thinking sadly that Evan, the survivor of a bitter and costly divorce battle, would run a mile once he heard about her mother's financial embarrassments. But, in all probability, nothing more than friendship would have developed between Beth and Evan, anyway, Tilda told herself in exasperation. Since when had she believed in fairy tales?

Her own workaholic father, whom she barely remembered, had been knocked down and killed by a drunk driver when she was five years old. Her mother's subsequent second marriage had been a disaster. Bullied and cowed by Scott, Beth had been in no fit state to protect her children. In Tilda's last year at school, her stepfather had made her work at night in a sleazy club run by one of his cronies.

Tilda forced her straying thoughts back to the present and scolded herself for that momentary slide back into the past. What was needed was action, not time-wasting regret for facts that could not be changed! She reached for the phone and rang the number of the legal firm on the letterhead to ask for an appointment. Humble pleading on the score of extreme urgency won her a late-morning slot the next day. Having arranged several days' leave from her current employment as an accounts assistant, she called her bank and asked how much money she would be allowed to borrow. Her worst fears were fulfilled when the loan officer pointed out that she had no assets and was still on probation in her current job. As she had never been a quitter she contacted three other financial institutions in the hope of receiving a more promising response before she accepted defeat on that issue.

The following day she put on a black trouser suit and caught a train to London. She made a punctual appearance at the imposing legal offices of Ratburn, Ratburn and Mildrop in the City. Ushered into the presence of an urbane, well-turned-out lawyer, she was tense and within minutes it seemed that every word she uttered was worthy only of a stony rebuttal.

'I'm unable to discuss your mother's confidential affairs with you, Miss Crawford.' An explanation of Beth's agoraphobia merely led to a further question. 'Unless, of course, you have acquired power of attorney to speak and act on Mrs Morrison's behalf?'

'No…but I was once quite friendly with Prince Rashad,' Tilda heard herself say, desperate to prove her credentials in some way and win a serious hearing.

The middle-aged lawyer dealt her a cool appraisal. 'I am not aware that His Royal Highness is involved in this matter.'

Tilda became even tenser. 'I appreciate that the loan was ostensibly advanced by a business called Metropolis—'

'I cannot discuss confidential matters with a third party.'

Her full soft mouth compressed. 'Then let me talk it over with Rashad direct. Please tell me how I can get in touch with him quickly.'

'I'm afraid that's not possible.' Before she could pursue the point, the older man stood up to signify that the meeting was at an end.

Less than two minutes later, Tilda was back out

on the street again. She was mortified by the reception she had received. She caught the bus to the opulent Embassy of Bakhar, where her request for a phone number or meeting with the Crown Prince was treated with a smiling but dismissive courtesy that gained her not a millimetre of access. The level of security and discretion that appeared to surround Rashad's movements was daunting. Direct contact with him was clearly not to be had for the asking. Her only option was to leave her phone number, which would be passed on to his staff. Throughout her unsatisfactory visit, she was quite unaware of a bearded older man with silvering hair, who had left his office the moment he had seen her name pop up on his computer screen. A troubled frown on his stolid features, he watched her depart from his vantage point on the landing above.

Determined not to be beaten in her quest, Tilda went straight to the nearest library and used the Internet. She was initially infuriated by the discovery that Rashad was currently in London and yet nobody had been prepared to admit that. But when she noticed the date of the charity benefit he was to attend and realised that it was being staged that very day, it lent wings to her thoughts and her feet.

At the reception desk of the exclusive hotel where the benefit was being held, Tilda learned that admission was by invitation only. She paid for an eye-wateringly expensive soft drink so that she could sit in the hotel foyer. Sophisticated women in fashionable cocktail frocks walked in and out of the crowded ballroom. A door was propped wide to facilitate the exit of a man in a wheelchair, and Tilda caught a glimpse of a very tall, powerful male standing about thirty feet inside the room.

Her heart lurched as if she had suddenly been thrown high in the air without warning. It was Rashad, and there was something so achingly familiar in the proud angle of his dark head that she rose to her feet without being aware of it. Her attention roved from the crisp luxuriance of his cropped black hair to the bold lineaments of his strong profile. Below the bright ballroom lights, his skin had the rich sheen of gold, showcasing his well-defined black brows, a thin aristocratic blade of a nose and a fierce sensual mouth set above a hard, masculine jaw line. He was incredibly good-looking in a very exotic, un-English way. Back in the days when she had innocently dreamt of a future as an artist, she had drawn his face over and over again, obsessively attached to every detail of his hawkish features that might have been lifted from an ancient Berber hanging.

He was surrounded by a circle of people. She was willing him to turn his handsome head and notice her at the same moment that she registered that candy-pink female fingernails rested on his arm. For a split second she could not credit that she had not immediately seen the gorgeous brunette in her flimsy short dress flashing an intimate smile up at him. It was as though Tilda's mind had censored that part of her view, only letting her see what she could handle. The last time she had seen Rashad in the flesh five years earlier he had also been with another woman, a sight that had ensured that an extra large dollop of humiliation had been added to her agonised sense of rejection.

Now, as then, pride and anger came to Tilda's rescue. Just as her eyes swerved back onto him, Rashad finally looked in her direction. His keen, dark-as-ebony gaze was trained on her. Not a muscle moved on his lean, strong face. He blanked her as if she didn't exist and her view was cut off as the door swung shut again. In shock at that lack of reaction, Tilda turned pale as death. She went back to Reception and asked to leave a message for Prince Rashad. She hovered while it was being delivered but the minutes ticked slowly past and no answer came back. She sat down again, hollow with physical hunger, for she had not eaten since early morning. But she had no option other than to wait. She dared not leave while there was still an ounce of hope that he might respond to her request for a meeting.

It was almost three hours before Rashad chose to make his departure. Several powerfully built

Arab men emerged from the function room and fanned out in an advance guard before Rashad strode into view. He had fantastic carriage, moving with the grace of a prowling panther. His sinuous female companion had to almost run to keep up in her high heels. Tilda could not have broken through the tight cordon of security that kept lesser mortals at bay in the royal presence. She watched as the paparazzi outside flashed cameras and shouted questions. Rashad ignored them and moved down the steps.

'Miss Crawford?'

A dark-skinned older man extended a card to her with a quiet nod and walked on out the door.

Blinking in surprise, Tilda studied the card, which contained an address and a time late the following afternoon. She sucked in a tremulous breath. Rashad was giving her the chance to plead her family's case. But if she had not dutifully waited all those hours like a lowly supplicant for His Royal Highness's attention, she would not have got the concession. Anger stirring afresh, she recognised how Rashad made her suffer: first the whip, then the reward—but only if appropriate humility was displayed.

Reclining back into the comfort of his limousine, Rashad thought about Tilda Crawford, defiantly clad in the sort of masculine clothes he had never liked. Why did she only dress up like that for his benefit? Nothing could detract from such striking natural beauty. Even with her mermaid's mass of curling pale blond hair tied back, her turquoise eyes and the heart-shaped pout of her full pink mouth bare of cosmetic enhancement, she had held every male eye in her vicinity.

Rashad had enjoyed keeping her waiting. He knew what kind of woman she was and he would give no quarter when he dealt with her. In truth, being very tough came naturally to Rashad, who had found restraint and tenderness a much greater challenge. While engaged in picturing Tilda he discovered that a sense of unlimited power could also act as an aphrodisiac. The eager brunette by his side rested a slim, caressing hand on his lean, powerful thigh. With a languid forefinger Rashad depressed the button to screen the windows....

CHAPTER TWO

Tilda sat rigid-backed on the crowded bus that carried her the last mile to her destination. Garbed in what her mother persisted in calling her 'Sunday best'—a long black coat that she wore every winter to go to church—she was striving not to let nerves get the better of her temper.

Unfortunately every time she recalled how Rashad had just *ignored* her at the hotel, a sense of grievance grew inside her. What had she ever done to deserve such discourteous treatment? After all, it was not as though she had even had the slightest suspicion that her mother had asked him for financial help. She pressed cold hands to her hot cheeks as though she could cool the mortified heat that that fact still awakened in her. The whole ghastly business was threatening to tear her apart.

Metropolis Enterprises was housed in a massive contemporary office block. The company comprised a long list of different businesses, which were displayed on the inaugural plaque in the foyer. The building had been officially opened by Prince Rashad Hussein Al-Zafar. She travelled up to the top floor in a glass lift. In the waiting area she sucked in a long desperate breath. For just a moment she thought she couldn't do it, couldn't face asking for time and understanding from a guy who had once torn her heart and her self-esteem to pieces.

'Miss Crawford—come this way.'

Tilda straightened her stiff shoulders and followed the male PA. She was shown into a very large but empty office. Barely had the door closed behind her, however, than another opened across the room and Rashad entered.

His raw physical impact hit her like a tidal wave that swept away rational thought. His fabulously tailored black pinstripe suit oozed designer style, emphasising his wide, powerful shoulders, lean hips and long straight legs. Her heart felt as though it were pounding like mad somewhere in the region of her throat. Meeting eyes as amber gold as a hot sunset, she found it equally hard to catch her breath. For her it was like time rolling back and her response was immediate: her mouth ran dry, her slender length tensing with anticipation. It had been five long years since she had experienced that unsettling little clenching sensation way down low in her tummy and it seriously rattled her.

Surveying her only for the space of a heartbeat, Rashad came to a prowling halt by his desk. His lean strong face hardened on the unwelcome reflection that she bore more than a passing resemblance to some divine snow maiden. The high-necked long black coat provided a dramatic frame for the delicate perfection of her ivory skin and light blond hair. Scarcely divine, he adjusted with inner cynicism, regardless of the purity of her looks. Naturally she knew the effect of her startling beauty. Naturally that aura of artless innocence was a façade designed to ensnare foolish men. He knew that better than anyone.

'Thank you for seeing me.' Tilda shot that at him a little breathlessly, determined to show that she had better manners than he had demonstrated at the hotel.

'Curiosity got to me,' Rashad confided lazily, watching her long honey-brown lashes flutter down over the astonishing turquoise of her eyes, the slight downward pout of her curvaceous pink lower lip. In point of fact, she was still exquisite. A few inches taller and she would have rivalled any supermodel. Five years ago, he had had excellent taste in so far as appearance alone counted. He wondered if she would dare to say no to him now were he to reach for her and, that fast, the stinging heavy heat of arousal engulfed his groin. He gritted his even white teeth at the shock of that instantaneous sexual reaction and killed the frivolous thought that had preceded it. It had not occurred to him that he might still respond to her even when his strong self-discipline and intelligence were in direct opposition to that weakness.

By dint of not quite looking directly at Rashad,

Tilda rescued what remained of her concentration and plunged straight to what she saw as the heart of the matter. 'I had no idea that my mother had asked you to loan her money when we were seeing each other. If I had known at the time I would have stopped you getting involved in our family problems.'

Rashad was tempted to laugh out loud at such an implausible claim. *As if!* He strode over to the window, presenting her with his bold chiselled profile. He supposed her ludicrous assertion of ignorance was yet one more example of her old habit of always pleading innocence or having a viable explanation to cover her tracks. The leopard, it seemed, had not changed her spots. Nothing was ever Tilda's fault or her responsibility.

Tilda moved closer in her eagerness to say all that she could in explanation before he could say anything. 'Mum shouldn't have asked you to help, but you shouldn't have given it, either,' she framed in an apologetic tone. 'I mean, how on earth did you ever believe she could pay such a huge amount back? Why didn't you at least tell me what you were thinking of doing before you did it?'

Rashad swung back to face her, for she was stretching credulity too far with that enquiry. A sardonic curve hardened his handsome mouth. 'Surely that wasn't part of your plan?'

Her delicate brows drew together in a slight frown of confusion. 'Plan? What plan? I don't know what you're talking about.'

Rashad surveyed her with derisive cool and he had to admit that she put on a very convincing act. That expression of mystification in her wide turquoise eyes would have persuaded most men that she was speaking the truth. Unhappily for her, past experience had fully armoured Rashad against the lies she might well tell in an effort to awaken his compassion.

The silence felt claustrophobic to Tilda. She did not understand what was wrong or why he had made no response, but she did recognize the scorn gleaming in his narrowed dark gaze. 'Why are you looking at me like that?'

'It astonishes me that you should dare to come into my presence and criticise my generosity towards your relatives. That might be a wily move with some men, but I find your reproaches offensive.'

Something in that clipped, dark tone chilled her to the marrow and her tension climbed even higher. 'I'm not denying your generosity and I have no wish to be offensive or ungrateful for the spirit that prompted you to give that money. But Mum had no reasonable prospect of ever repaying you and that should have made you think twice about what you were doing.'

His expressive mouth curled. 'Your mother was offered the option of paying rent.'

Tilda recognised that the meeting was already going badly wrong and feared that she was letting her personal pride and animosity get in the way of making a proper clarification of the facts. 'A lot has changed in our lives over the last five years, Rashad. My stepfather has gone. For a while, we lived in chaos. I'm afraid that my mother now suffers from—'

'Stop right there,' Rashad commanded with razor-sharp clarity. 'I have no desire to listen to maudlin sob stories. We are not players in a soap opera, nor do we have a personal relationship. We are dealing with a business matter. Respect those boundaries.'

At that uncompromising rebuke, mortified colour mantled Tilda's cheeks. Sob stories? Was that how her references to her family's plight had struck him five years ago? When she had confided in him, had he viewed her trust in him as an inappropriate and unwelcome demand for sympathy? Yet not once had she told him about the serious shortage of money within her home! In the same way she had been too ashamed to admit that her stepfather was a good deal worse than just a work-shy bully and, indeed, had a criminal record.

'Yes, I appreciate that, but—'

'Do not interrupt me when I am speaking. It is very rude,' Rashad sliced back without hesitation.

'I was only trying to explain my mother's position and why she has allowed this situation to get out of hand.' Annoyed by that reprimand,

Tilda had to make a real effort to remain focused and resist the urge to fight back in self-defence. But keeping her head was very difficult when Rashad was behaving like a stranger. It was a challenge to believe that he had ever been anything else. His English had become much more idiomatic and his manner towards her was brutally cold and distant. She had never been more conscious of his royal birth and background. Yet she still found it remarkably hard not to stare at him for his sheer strength of character had always drawn her even when she was struggling bone and sinew to resist him. Her painful awareness of just how much he had once hurt her was doing nothing to stabilise her emotions.

'Mrs Morrison's personal circumstances are irrelevant,' Rashad declared. 'Five years have passed. There has not been a single attempt to service the loan advanced for the settlement of her debts, nor has there been rent paid according to the tenancy agreement. Such an abysmal record speaks for itself.'

As Rashad reminded Tilda of those embarrassing realities an uncomfortable flush washed her fair complexion. 'I recognise that Mum has dealt with all this very badly, but unfortunately I wasn't aware until this week that you owned the house and had also loaned her money.'

At that declaration, his lean bronzed features took on a forbidding aspect. 'Another unlikely excuse? It is hard to credit that you believe the same scam could work twice.'

'*Scam?*' Tilda echoed with an uncertain laugh. 'What scam?'

'Did you think I wouldn't appreciate five years ago that you were doing everything you could to profit from our relationship? It was a scam aimed at milking my interest in you for as much money as you could get. You softened me up with your tear-jerking tales and very prettily you did it. Then your mother begged me to help her to protect you and your siblings from your evil stepfather's spendthrift ways!'

Tilda studied him in horror. 'I just can't believe that you can think that of me or Mum! I only ever told you the truth. I did not try to *milk* your interest in me—what a disgusting term!'

'What else did you do? Nor are your sensibilities as refined as you like to pretend. Why don't we look at the facts? When I first met you, you were working in a bar and dancing in a cage.'

Her turquoise eyes flashed with the blue-gold of a flame in the hottest part of the fire. Temper leapt up so high inside her that she was momentarily left breathless by the impact. Her slim white hands clenched into fists. 'I wondered when you were going to get around to mentioning that again. Since when was bar work on a level with prostitution? I wasn't a lap dancer or a stripper. The one time in my life I danced in a cage for a couple of hours and you never let me live it down!' she launched at him furiously. 'I should never have got involved with you. You were prejudiced against me from the start!'

Brilliant dark eyes gleamed warning gold beneath the lush black fringe of his lashes. 'The past is not up for discussion—'

'Except when it's you making a point?' Tilda was seething at the humiliation of having that ghastly cage episode flung in her teeth five years after the event. So much for Rashad acting like a stranger! Rashad, she thought suddenly, hadn't changed one little bit. He could always be depended on to remind her of the worst possible moments in her life. 'I'm not an immoral or dishonest or greedy person and I never have been!'

Rashad was dimly surprised to register that he was enjoying himself. She was the only woman who had ever dared to raise her voice in his vicinity or tried to argue with him. Once that trait had thoroughly irritated him but now he recognised it for the novelty and the weakness it was. His self-discipline absolute, he elevated a winged ebony brow in mocking encouragement. 'Is that so?'

'Of course it is…' Tilda pushed a trembling hand through the silky stray curls clinging to her warm forehead. 'For some reason you've put together a whole nasty scenario that didn't happen. There was never any plan to get money off you.'

'So…why, in your considered opinion, am I half a million pounds poorer from having known you?'

When Rashad mentioned that particular sum, consternation knocked the breath and the temper out of Tilda. 'Half…a million pounds?' she whispered shakily.

'The sale of the house will recoup some of that loss and the property has at least appreciated as an asset,' Rashad drawled with a complete calm that she found extremely threatening. 'But I assume the rent will never be paid and as for the loan—'

'It can't all come to half a million pounds!' Tilda gasped strickenly.

'Rather more. That is a conservative quote,' Rashad delivered drily. 'I'm surprised that you haven't already worked out the exact amount. I seem to recall that you have a head for figures as good as any calculator.'

Her soft full mouth pursed for she could recognise an insult no matter how well veiled it was. 'But I haven't had access to all the documentation involved.'

'In your role as innocent bystander, naturally not,' Rashad slotted in with an unconcealed derision as frank as a shout of disbelief. 'No matter, I intend to reclaim the debt in full.'

Realising that events were running on without her, Tilda was in a panic. 'You mustn't. If you were willing to give us more time—'

'Until the *next* millennium?'

'Why do you have such a low opinion of me?' Frustration pounded through Tilda, her eyes bright with angry incomprehension again. 'I understand that my family comes out of this looking like freeloaders, but when you won't even let me explain *why*—'

Intent dark golden eyes, heavily enhanced by spiky black lashes, slammed coolly into hers. 'Let's stick to business.'

'OK. In one more year I hope to be fully qualified as an accountant.'

Rashad raised a brow in surprise. 'How novel…when you were with me, all you could talk about was being an artist.'

It was on the tip of her tongue to point out that

the need to earn a living and help her mother raise her siblings had soon put paid to that prospect. She had had to give up her place at art college and find a job instead. But that was not a sacrifice she had ever questioned or regretted.

'I have the ability to earn a decent salary and start paying back what is owed,' Tilda swore with an urgency that betrayed the depth of her concern.

'You have an English saying. A bird in the hand is worth two in the bush. Promises are not of interest to me. If you have nothing more concrete to offer, one might wonder why you went to so much trouble to bring about this meeting,' Rashad drawled, soft and smooth as silk. 'At least, if I didn't know you I might wonder. Knowing you as I do, however, I suspect that you hoped to use your sex appeal as a bargaining chip.'

Tilda was so hugely taken aback by that unjust accusation that her soft mouth opened and shut again. Her coat and her boots covered her head to toe and she wasn't even wearing make-up. There was nothing provocative about her outfit.

How did he think she should have presented herself? With a paper bag over her head and her body wrapped in a sack? Pure outrage lit her luminous blue-green gaze. 'How dare you suggest that?'

'But that's what you do. Five years ago you were very careful to withhold your body and play the virgin card to keep me interested.'

Absorbing those words, Tilda breathed in so deep she was vaguely surprised that she didn't spontaneously combust in front of him. 'So this is what you call sticking to business, is it?'

Grim dark golden eyes clashed with hers. 'But I *was* a business proposition as far as you were concerned. You set out to rip me off.'

Tilda snatched in a jerky breath. 'That's outrageous!'

'But true, nonetheless, and if you haven't come here to settle the outstanding debt or at least tender a substantial part of it, why *are* you here?' Rashad enquired very drily.

Her hands clenched into tight fists of restraint for she recognised how he had backed her into a corner and cut off every avenue of escape. If she told the truth and admitted that she had hoped to awaken his compassion by explaining her mother's circumstances, she would vindicate his accusation about her telling sob stories for profit. Her even white teeth set together. 'I hoped that you would give us more time to pay.'

Rashad strolled soundlessly towards her, his pronounced elegance of carriage contriving to hook her attention against her will. But then the very first thing that she had ever noticed about Rashad was the fluid, impossibly sexy grace of his every physical movement. At that memory a tiny betraying little quiver darted through her tummy, tensing her every muscle with defensiveness.

'On what basis would I grant a request for more time?' Rashad drawled lazily. 'I'm a businessman. If you can't raise the money now, there is little chance that you could produce it in the near future.'

'You weren't behaving like a businessman when you commented on the fact that I didn't sleep with you five years ago!' Tilda suddenly shot at him, fed up of playing the game solely by his rules. 'You are totally biased against me!'

Rashad strolled closer. He was so much taller that Tilda felt overshadowed by his proximity. 'Don't waste my time trying to distract me from the issue. I will ask you again—why are you here?'

A faint aromatic hint of sandalwood caught at Tilda's throat and her nostrils and threatened to send her spiralling down into a rich tide of recollection. She was trying to avoid meeting his dark golden gaze, but she could feel his scrutiny and it was as if heat pulsed wherever his brilliant eyes chose to rest. Her mouth tingled, her slender throat tightened. A languorous heaviness was seeping up through her lower limbs, coiling in her belly and sending fingers of awareness darting through her small full breasts.

'For goodness' sake, you know why I'm here,' she argued half under her breath. Being that close to him made her feel dominated and she took a swift step back.

Every imperious line of his lithe hard body taut with command and impatience, Rashad was determined to strip her bare of her manipulative pretences. He closed the distance between them again. 'From my point of view it would appear that you have approached me with nothing to offer but yourself.'

Hot pink flooded her cheeks and she was startled into a swift upward glance. She was so conscious of his potent authority and strength that she continued to back away from him without even being aware of what she was doing. 'What on earth is that supposed to mean?' she queried half an octave higher.

'I don't think you're that naïve.'

Taut with wrathful incredulity as he confirmed that he meant what she had assumed he could not possibly dare to suggest, Tilda stared up at him, turquoise eyes bright as jewels. 'Are you suggesting that I would try to offer you *sex?*' she gasped.

Cynical amusement filled Rashad, for she acted the affronted virgin with such perfection. 'In the absence of any other option, what else is there?'

At that cruelly mocking confirmation, the anger inside Tilda just cut loose of her restraint and she tried to slap him. But unfortunately her victim had far faster responses and he caught her wrist in midair. 'No... I don't tolerate tantrums!'

'Let go of me!' Tilda gritted in a tempest of fury at having been both insulted and denied any right of reprisal.

'Not until you calm down.' Rashad retained a firm hold on her narrow wrist. He was angry with her but there was a dark, insidious excitement beginning to stir, as well. A desire for what he had once been denied, he told himself harshly. Yet why should he censure himself for what were only natural promptings? He had a powerful libido and she was a very beautiful woman. A mere seventy years earlier, his grandfather had enjoyed a harem of concubines. For a split second, Rashad allowed himself to imagine what it would be like to have Tilda Crawford entirely at his disposal at any hour of the day. *His alone.* The images that assailed him were so compellingly evocative that they were dispelled only with the greatest difficulty.

'I said—let go!' Tilda was so mad at being held captive like a disobedient child that she attempted to kick him. As he evaded that new potential angle of assault she yanked herself free with a suddenness that sent her careening into the piece of furniture behind her. With a yelp of dismay she fell over the coffee-table and landed on her behind on the other side of it with a loud thump.

'Is it not time that you learned how to control your temper?' With smouldering dark golden eyes, Rashad surveyed her lying in tumbled disarray on his office carpet. He strode forward, reached down and pulled her upright again in one easy motion. 'Are you hurt?'

'No.' Stiff with shame and embarrassment at her loss of control in the presence of the enemy, Tilda shook her head. She tried to make herself apologise and, unfortunately, the words were strangled at the back of her throat. At that moment she hated him with a passion. Yet she had only to connect with his brilliant gaze for a heartbeat to feel the stark rise of yearning that slaughtered her pride.

Rashad studied her lush raspberry-pink mouth and remembered the soft sweet taste of it. He allowed his imagination full sway while he asked himself why he should not turn fantasy into fact. *Tilda at his disposal.* Unleashed from his habitual rigid self-discipline, fierce arousal licked like blazing flames of fire at his lithe, muscular frame. Almost as quickly he reached a decision. He would indulge himself with her. He would indulge his every desire with her until he was sated of that pale blonde perfection.

Why should he not take her? Would it not be the natural justice that he was entitled to claim? Why should he consider the question of honour with a woman of her reputation? He knew what she was. Somewhere he still had the security file that had destroyed his youthful illusions. While he had been with her, she had lied to him, deceived him and slept with other men. Rashad had learnt to his cost that fine principles were a serious weakness and a handicap around Tilda Crawford.

Startlingly aware of the buzz in the tense atmosphere, Tilda was trembling. As she took a step back her hips hit the wall and she braced her slim shoulders against it, gathering up her courage. 'I wasn't offering you sex,' she told him defensively.

Rashad surveyed her with glittering intensity. 'It's the only thing you have to give that I want.'

The silence pulsed and vibrated.

'Are you mad?' Barely able to credit that Rashad could admit that shocking truth to her without betraying even a glimmer of shame, Tilda sucked in a shuddering breath. 'I refuse to believe that you're serious! Sex in return for money? How can you insult me to that extent?'

'Most women consider my attentions an honour. The choice is yours.' His stunning golden gaze narrowed to a smouldering glitter, Rashad let a long brown forefinger push up her chin so that their eyes could meet. 'Make the right choice and you will discover that I can make repayment the sweetest of pleasures.'

Tilda was even more taken aback when that low-pitched forecast made her mouth run dry and butterflies break loose in her tummy. She could not dredge her attention from his lean, strong face or the shimmering gold of his stare. He lowered his arrogant dark head and a pulse beat like a drum pounded through her, leaving every inch of her tense as a drawn bow with anticipation. A little voice told her to move away, raise a hand to keep him away from her, even angle her head back out of reach. She heard the voice but she stayed put, controlled by much more powerful influences. His mouth came down on hers in a slow, languorous tasting that unleashed a host of sensations that she had forced herself to forget. It was a ravishingly potent kiss. Her breasts felt full and constrained by her clothing. A shivery little frisson of wicked delight ran through her slender figure and stirred a deep ache of hunger between her thighs.

Reacting to that shattering response with horror-stricken recoil, Tilda pulled back and spluttered, 'No, thank you very much! Once burnt, twice shy!'

Stunning eyes veiled, Rashad surveyed her with satisfaction.

'So you can still kiss up a storm!' Tilda launched at him furiously. 'But you should be ashamed of yourself for treating me like this!'

Rashad consulted the rapier thin designer watch on his wrist and murmured with smooth regret, 'I have another appointment now. Your time is up.'

'Oh, don't you worry—I'm going all right!' Tilda spun on her heel and hauled open the door with a perspiring palm.

Rashad sent her a sardonic smile. 'You really couldn't expect me to fall for the same fairy stories this time around.'

Her oval face red as fire, Tilda stalked out.

CHAPTER THREE

TILDA got on the train back to Oxford. She was in shock. Everything about her meeting with Rashad had shaken her up. Not least the manner in which she had reacted to that kiss! Her passionate physical response to him had coursed through her like a river in flood and she was furious with herself. Evidently loathing Prince Rashad Hussein Al-Zafar was no defence whatsoever against his persuasive sensuality. What did that say about her intelligence or her self-control?

In that field, Tilda conceded angrily, absolutely nothing had changed in five wretched years. Rashad had still only to touch her to set her on fire with longing. But nobody knew better than

Tilda that it was a kind of weakness that could lead to disaster. Her family history bore that out. Her mother, Beth, had only been nineteen when she had fallen pregnant with Tilda and had had to get married in a hurry. Beth's woes had not ended there for her husband had resented his new family obligations. An ambitious young lawyer, he had been a neglectful husband and an uninterested parent. Five years later, Beth had become a widow and an easy mark for Scott Morrison's promises of undying devotion. Madly in love, Beth had conceived her third child just a few months into the relationship and had rushed back into marriage with seriously unhappy results.

Tilda suppressed a sigh. Although she felt guilty acknowledging it, she had tried to learn by her mother's mistakes and had resolved that no man would ever be allowed to come between her and her wits, or her education, for that matter. In the early teenage years she had had little interest in boys. Scott's bullying, drinking and womanising had put her off the entire male sex, while she had done what she could to support her mother and help out with the younger children.

At eighteen years old, she had been in her last year of school. When Scott had told her that he had fixed her up with part-time work as a waitress in a nightclub managed by one of his seedy friends she had been incensed, for she had already had a weekend job in a supermarket. Unfortunately whenever Tilda had dared to defy Scott, he had taken his temper out on the rest of her family, who had been much less able to stand up to him. Within a week the continual arguments and her mother's distress had vanquished Tilda's resistance. While dutifully agreeing with Beth that, yes, she would earn more money, she had known that the extra hours and late nights would scarcely be conducive to the intensive studying she had been doing for her final exams.

From the outset Tilda had hated the attention that her looks had drawn from the customers. The club had attracted slick, high-earning professionals and wealthy students and spoilt young men who had drunk too much and thought the female staff were fair game. Tilda had soon realised why the manager only seemed to hire waitresses who were more than ordinarily attractive. Some of them had regularly slept with the clientele in return for gifts or cash and their liberal ways had encouraged custom.

Tilda had worked there only a fortnight before she had first seen Rashad. His supple, sexy aura as he had descended the stairs had caught her eye first. When he had turned his head and locked dark golden eyes with hers, she had literally stopped breathing. Mentally it had been like running into a solid brick wall and seeing stars. She had found it impossible not to keep gazing around to see where he was, or to steal another transfixed glance at him. Every time she had looked, she had found that he was looking, too, and, even though that had embarrassed her, she had been helpless to resist temptation.

A big dark-haired guy had approached her towards the end of that evening. 'Fancy coming to a party tonight?' he asked, his foreign accent roughening his pronunciation.

'No, thanks,' she said flatly, turning away.

'I'm Leonidas Pallis and I have a friend who wants to meet you.' He dropped a card and a hundred pound note down on the tray she was holding. 'Party kicks off around midnight. That should cover your cab fare.'

'I said, no, thanks.' Her cheeks scarlet, Tilda thrust the banknote back at him and walked away.

Soon afterwards, a waitress called Chantal came over to speak to her. 'You really riled Leonidas. Don't you know who he is? He's the grandson of a Greek tycoon and he's absolutely loaded. He gives incredible tips and throws amazing parties. What's your problem?'

'I'm just not interested in mixing with the customers outside working hours.' Tilda could also have mentioned that she had school the next day, but the manager had banned her from admitting that she was still a schoolgirl as he had said it might give the club a bad name.

When she emerged into the car park at closing time, a surprising number of vehicles were still there. She heard a vigorous burst of male laughter. Her heart sank when she spotted the Greek guy drinking from a bottle and leaning up against the bonnet of a Ferrari with his mates. Then she saw Rashad straightening up and moving towards her. Something very like panic gripped her but her feet were frozen to the spot. He was so stunningly handsome she was mesmerised by the clean, hard-boned lines of lean dark features.

'I'm Rashad,' he murmured softly, and he extended his hand with a formality that took her entirely by surprise.

'Tilda,' she breathed, just touching his lean brown fingers.

'May I drive you home?'

'I get a lift with one of the other girls.'

Unexpectedly, Rashad smiled as if such an explanation was perfectly acceptable to him. 'Of course. It is very late. Will you give me your phone number?'

That charismatic smile threatened her defences and she battened down the hatches, terrified of what he was making her feel. 'No, sorry. I don't date club members.'

The following evening the club manager, Pete, cornered her. 'I hear you blew away our new royal VIP last night,' he accused.

'Royal?' Tilda parroted, wide-eyed.

'Prince Rashad, the heir to the throne of Bakhar and a string of oil wells.' Pete dealt her an angry look. 'Our two best customers— Leonidas Pallis and Sergio Torrente—brought him in. Those guys are minted, too. They spend thousands here and I don't want any stupid little girl offending them. Is that clear?'

'But I haven't done anything.'

'Do yourself a favour. Smile sweetly and give the prince your phone number.'

Pete changed the table rota so that, on her next shift, Tilda was serving the VIP table. Now that she knew who Rashad was, she noticed his thickset bodyguards trying unsuccessfully to stay in the background. Uneasily aware of his royal status, she tried very hard to put him out of her mind. But he dominated her every thought and response. It was as if an invisible wire attached her to him, so that she noticed his every tiny move. In comparison with him, his companions were immature. He seemed to be the only one of the group graced with morals or manners. He didn't drink to excess, he didn't fool around, he was always courteous. He was also absolutely, totally gorgeous and it did not escape her attention that every girl in the place had her eye on him.

The night she tripped and dropped a tray of drinks, everything changed. While his rowdy mates laughed at the spectacle she made, Rashad sprang to his feet and immediately helped her up from the floor.

'You are unhurt?'

Her hand trembled in his and she connected with brilliant dark eyes enhanced by luxuriant ebony lashes.

'When you fell my heart stopped beating,' he breathed in a raw undertone.

That was the moment she went from being infatuated with his vibrant dark good looks to falling head over heels in love with him, but she still pulled her hand free with muffled thanks and hurriedly walked away. She saw it as being sensible and protecting herself from a broken heart. What future was there in loving a guy who was only a temporary visitor to her country and, even worse, destined to be a king? His two friends approached her later that evening. Making it clear that the shy stolen glances that betrayed her attraction to Rashad had not passed unnoticed, Leonidas and Sergio virtually accused her of being a tease.

'How much do you want to go out with him?' Leonidas demanded contemptuously, peeling off notes from the thick wad in his wallet.

'You're not rich enough!' Tilda snapped in disgust.

She went home in tears that night only to find her stepfather, Scott, drunkenly upbraiding her mother with the club manager, Pete's, complaint that Tilda had an unfriendly attitude towards the customers. The next weekend Pete told her that she had to stand in for one of the cage dancers who had called in sick. She refused. Threatened with the sack and worn down by what felt like everybody's criticisms, she gave way, reasoning that the bikini-style outfit exposed no more than she would have revealed at the swimming pool. She persuaded herself that nobody really looked at the dancers except as gyrating bodies that added to the club atmosphere.

When Rashad arrived, a birthday cake was brought in for his benefit. Tilda still recalled the instant when he had registered who was dancing in the cage: the shock and consternation, the distaste he had been unable to hide. In the same moment cage dancing had gone from being what Tilda had told herself was essentially harmless to the equivalent of dancing naked and shame- less in the street. When Rashad studiously averted his attention from her as though she were putting on an indecent display, she fled from the cage and refused to get back into it again. Chantal later revealed that Tilda had been set up.

'It's the prince's twenty-fifth birthday. Sergio and Leonidas thought it would be a laugh to get you into the cage. They paid Pete to fix it for them.'

Tilda never did tell Rashad that truth. Telling tales about his best friends wouldn't have got her very far. Instead, she blamed herself for not having had the guts to tell Pete where to get off. Eyes red from tears, she put on her uniform and got on with her usual waitressing. Already promised a full-time summer job at the firm owned by Evan Jerrold, she consoled herself with the prayerful hope that she would not be serving drinks for much longer. Unhappily, however, new employment would mean that she was unlikely to ever see Rashad again.

When she finished her shift, she emerged from the club to find the weather was wet and unseasonably cold, and that the girl who usually gave her a lift had gone off to a party without telling her. Shivering while she was trying to call a cab on her mobile, she tensed when a silver Aston Martin Vanquish pulled up in front of her with a throaty growl. Rashad sprang out and studied her in silence across the bonnet and she knew he wouldn't ask anything of her because he had asked before and she had said no. He was too proud to ask again. Tears made her eyes smart; she still felt so utterly humiliated that she had let herself be pressed into dancing in the cage.

As Rashad walked round the bonnet and reached out to open the passenger door one of his bodyguards skidded up at speed to do it for him and prevent him from lowering himself to such a mundane task.

'Thanks,' she said gruffly and got in. At that moment she was not aware of having made a decision. She just couldn't muster the mental resistance to walk away from him again. She told herself that if she kept things as light as though it were a holiday romance she wouldn't get hurt.

'You'll have to tell me where you live,' Rashad murmured as calmly as if she had been getting into his car every night for months.

'Happy birthday,' she said in a wobbly voice, as the excessively emotional surge of tears was still threatening her composure.

At the traffic lights he reached for her hand and almost crushed it within the fierce hold of his. 'In my country we stopped putting people in cages when slavery was outlawed a hundred years ago.'

'I shouldn't have agreed to do it.'

'You did not wish to?'

'Of course not—apart from anything else, I'm not a dancer.'

'Don't do it again,' Rashad told her with innate authority and instantly she wanted to do it again just to demonstrate her independence. She had to bite her lip not to respond with the defiance that she had acquired to hold her own with her stepfather.

And so it began: a relationship that attracted a great deal of unwelcome comment from others. Leonidas Pallis made it clear that he regarded her in much the same light as a call-girl. Sergio Torrente, the sleek, sophisticated Italian who completed the trio of friends, seemed equally disdainful of Tilda's right to be treated with respect, but was not quite so obvious about revealing the fact. Had she been less green about the strength of male bonding, she might have realised then that with such powerful enemies her relationship with Rashad was utterly doomed to end in tears.

As the hateful Leonidas Pallis put it, 'Why can't you keep it simple?' Tilda heard him ask Rashad this during a night out. 'Boy meets girl, boy shags girl, boy dumps girl. You don't romance waitresses!'

As her revolting stepfather put it: 'Well, you can thank me for getting you the job that's about to make your fortune. Tell him you like cash better than diamonds.'

Offered the chance to rent a room in a student house for the summer, she grabbed it to escape Scott and quit working at the club. At the same time she started her temporary job in the accounts department at Jerrold Plastics. The weeks that followed were the happiest but also the stormiest of her life, because Rashad laid down the law as if he were her commanding officer and did not adapt well to disagreement.

She was challenged to keep his hands off her, but whenever passion threatened to overcome prudence she backed off fast. She was a virgin, well aware that she came from a very fertile line of women, and she was totally terrified of getting pregnant. She honestly believed, too, that keeping serious sex out of the equation would lessen the pain when Rashad returned to Bakhar.

Tilda was yanked out of those unsettling recollections only when the train pulled into the station. While she queued for the bus, she began putting the recent knowledge she had gained into those memories and she winced at the picture that began to emerge. Although she had had no idea of it, there had been a whole hidden dimension to her relationship with Rashad. That financial aspect encompassed, not only the embarrassing level of her family's indebtedness, but also a seemingly brazen reluctance on her family's part to pay rent or pay off the loan. Was it any wonder that over time Rashad had become suspicious of her motives and decided that all along she must have been a gold-digger out for all she could get?

Sex... *It's the only thing you have to give that I want.* Still outraged by that declaration, Tilda could find no excuse for him on that score. Obviously that was all he had ever wanted from her and the brutal way he had ditched her had spelt out the same message. She was proud of the fact that she had not slept with Rashad five years earlier. But just as swiftly the false courage of offended pride and anger started to wane in the face of reality. When she began walking down the road where she lived her steps got slower and slower as she neared her home. After all, what had she achieved? She had got nowhere with Rashad. He was tough, resolute and ruthless. Emotion never got in the way of his self-discipline. Sadly, the strength, intellect and tenacity that she had once admired also made Rashad a lethally effective opponent.

Tilda was wrenched from her reflections by the startling sight of her former stepfather climbing into his beat-up car outside her home. As the older man had never demonstrated the smallest interest in maintaining contact with Katie, James and Megan, his three children by her mother, Tilda was taken aback. 'What are you doing here?' she asked in dismay.

'Mind your own bloody business!' Scott Morrison told her, his heavy face flushed with aggression below his thinning blond hair.

Seriously concerned, Tilda watched him shoot his vehicle back out onto the road. Why had he been visiting the house? He had come at a time when her mother would be alone. She went straight into Beth's workroom. Her mother was sobbing and the room was in turmoil. Curtains were heaped on the floor in a tangle and a chair had been turned over. Perhaps most telling of all, the older woman's purse lay open on the ironing board with only a few coins spilling out of it.

'I bumped into Scott outside. Has he been taking money off you again?' Tilda asked baldly.

Beth broke down and, piece by horrible piece, the whole story came tumbling out. When Scott had found out several years earlier that Rashad was the current owner of the house, he had accused Beth of defrauding him of his share of the property. Ever since then Beth had been living in fear of Scott's visits and giving way to his threats and demands for money. While she soothed the distraught older woman, Tilda's anger grew for she finally understood why Beth had found it impossible even to pay rent. From behind the scenes, Scott Morrison had still been bleeding Tilda's family dry.

'Scott got what he was entitled to when the divorce settlement went through the court. He has no right to anything more. He's been telling you lies. I'm going to get the police, Mum—'

'No, you can't do that.' Beth gave her a look of horror. 'Katie and James would die of shame if their father was arrested—'

'No, they'd die of shame at what's been going on here, what you've been putting up with on their behalf! Silence protects bullies like Scott. Don't you worry…I'll sort him out,' Tilda swore, furious with herself for not even suspecting what had been going on behind all their backs. The divorce had not gotten rid of Scott after all and working for a living had never been his way.

She was hanging her coat below the stairs when she noticed that the post had arrived. She tensed at the sight of the familiar brown envelope and scooped it up. Yes, just as she had feared it *was* yet another missive from Rashad's solicitors. Taking a deep breath, she tore it open. Nervous perspiration broke out on her brow as she realised what the letter was. It was a written notice asking her mother to leave the house within fourteen days. As the rent was in arrears the landlord, it stated, would go to court seeking possession at the end of the month.

Tilda took the letter upstairs. She just could not face giving it to her mother at that moment. From the window she watched her sisters, seventeen-year-old Katie and nine-year-old Megan, walking up the drive in their school uniforms. James was shambling along in their wake, a tall gangling boy of fourteen, who had still to grow into his very large feet and deep bass voice. Her brother, Aubrey, currently in his fourth year of studying medicine, would be home later. Tilda was deeply attached to all of her siblings. They had gone through so much unhappiness when Scott had been making their lives hell but they had stayed close. They were good kids, hard-working and sensible. What would losing their home mean to them? *Everything.* It would shatter her family, because Beth's agoraphobia would ensure that the older woman could not cope. When Beth fell apart at the seams, what then? Aubrey would probably drop out of med school and Katie would find it impossible to study for her A-levels.

There was only one way out, only one way of protecting her family from the horror of being put out on the street: Rashad.

Rashad…and sex. It would most probably be a major disappointment to Rashad, whose wom-anising exploits filled endless pages in the tabloid newspapers, to discover that Tilda did not possess a single special sexy talent to offer in the bedroom. Nothing but ignorance. It would serve him right, Tilda reflected, tight-mouthed. Even so, common sense urged that she would have to ensure that he wrote off all the debts and the house as well before it dawned on him that she really wasn't worth the sacrifice of that much money. She shuddered, shame enveloping her from head to toe. She would be selling herself like a product in return for cash.

She reminded herself that if she hadn't been so fearful of heartache and pregnancy, she would have ended up in bed with Rashad while she had been dating him. But it would have been different back then, because she had truly loved him and had certainly believed that he had more feelings for her than he had finally demonstrated. Would she be able to have sex just for the sake of it? Presumably other women did. There was no point being over-sensitive to the reality that she really had no choice if she wanted to protect the people she loved from having their lives devastated.

Standing by the window, she called Metropolis Enterprises on her mobile and asked to speak to Rashad. Various very well-trained personnel tried to head her off and make her settle for much smaller fry. She persisted with the reminder that she'd had an appointment with the prince earlier that day and added that he would be very annoyed if he did not receive her personal call.

Rashad was in a meeting when the message flashed up on his BlackBerry. *Tilda.* A slow, chilling smile curved his wide, handsome mouth as he took the call in his office. So, the fish was biting. He felt like a shark about to attend a banquet. She was his. Finally his to enjoy. At his leisure in a place of his choosing and for as long as he wanted her. He would make all the rules and she would really, really hate that. His brilliant dark golden eyes gleamed with anticipation. He pictured her greeting him when he returned from a long trip abroad and knew instantly where he would accommodate her. Somewhere where her talent for infidelity could not possibly be exercised. A discreet location where she had nothing to do but devote herself to being his sexual entertainment. He could think of no place more suitable than his late grandfather's desert palace.

'How may I be of assistance?' Rashad drawled smoother than the most expensive silk in tone.

Instantly Tilda wanted to reach down the phone and slap him, for she knew that he knew exactly why she was ringing. She swallowed her pride with difficulty. 'I'm willing to accept your offer.'

'What offer?'

Her short upper lip dampened with perspiration. 'You said it was the only thing I had to offer that you wanted.'

'Your body,' Rashad filled in gently, savouring every syllable. 'You. We'll have to meet to discuss the rules.'

'What rules?' she protested. 'I just want to know that that eviction order won't proceed.'

'Meet me tomorrow afternoon at my town house.' He quoted the address and a time. 'We'll sort out the details of our future association. You'll be living abroad. I can tell you that now.'

As Tilda parted her lips to argue with that alarmingly unexpected assurance, Rashad concluded drily, 'It will be as I say.'

At that juncture he terminated the call. He would not compromise on any point. The rules would not be negotiable. Everything would be as he wanted it to be. The sooner she learned that and accepted it, the better.

CHAPTER FOUR

EVAN JERROLD brought his elegant Jaguar car to a halt in the exclusive London residential square. 'Good luck,' he said cheerfully.

'Thank you.' Tilda opened the passenger door of the luxury vehicle with a sense of relief, since telling lies made her uncomfortable. Evan had offered her a lift when her mother had mentioned that Tilda was heading to London that afternoon. Asked why she was taking time out of work, Tilda had told the first fib that had occurred to her—that she was attending a job interview. It had then occurred to her that the excuse of a new job could well be the perfect cover, if Rashad stuck to his insistence that she travel abroad.

'Now remember I'll give you an excellent reference. I'll call back in an hour because you may be finished by then,' Evan told her.

Tilda was embarrassed. 'There's no need.'

The older man gave her a wry smile. 'If I have to drop you home again, it'll give me another excuse to see your mother. Don't think I haven't noticed that her spirits are very low just now.'

Clambering out of the car, Tilda almost winced at his insight, grateful that her siblings were less perceptive. She mounted the steps to the imposing front door, nerves leaping through her like jumping beans that couldn't settle.

'Tilda!' Evan called after her. 'You forgot your bag.'

Tilda hurried back down the steps to take it from him, apologising and thanking him in one urgent breath. Admitted to the town house by a manservant, she was shown to a seat in the large stylish hall. She wondered if Rashad's household staff still routinely greeted his every appearance on bended knee, touching their very brows to the floor in the need to demonstrate respect to the heir to the throne. A couple of minutes later, a bearded older man with greying hair appeared and came to a sudden halt at the sight of her, an expression of surprise skimming his thin intelligent face. With a scrupulously polite dipping of his head in acknowledgement of her presence, he walked past her and went out.

Tilda was ushered upstairs into a very grand drawing room. She was pleased to note that the manservant bowed rather than knelt. 'Miss Crawford, Your Royal Highness.'

Rashad surveyed her with dark eyes as cold as Arctic ice. Clad in a casual grey hooded jacket and black trousers, she should have looked ordinary. But the unassuming clothes simply accentuated her beauty and the slender grace of her figure. Several irrepressible curls were already springing loose above her brow with a silvery fair abundance that hinted at the full glory of her hair when it was worn loose. Memories stirred and, with the image, a surge of arousal, which he rigorously sought to control.

'Take a seat,' Rashad told her huskily.

Eyes bright as slivers of pure turquoise above

cheekbones stung pink by the spring breeze, Tilda shot him an edgy glance. Once again he was formally dressed in a superb charcoal-grey business suit teamed with a white shirt and a cobalt-blue silk tie. He looked amazingly handsome. And grim. Well, that was at least familiar, she told herself in an effort to gain control of herself. Rashad in censorious mode was nothing new to Tilda. When she had been dating him, she had sometimes felt as if he was putting her through a meticulous self-improvement programme. Feeling uncomfortably warm, she unbuttoned her jacket, removed it and sat down stiffly in an armchair.

'It was tasteless to allow your current lover to bring you here,' Rashad said with derision, 'but very much in line with the kind of childish defiance I expect from you.'

Tilda drew in some oxygen to steady herself and focused on his hand-stitched shoes. *Childish?* She reminded herself of the eviction order and of the vast amount of money outstanding and told herself that a few insults wouldn't hurt her. On the other hand, wrong assumptions had to be righted. 'Evan is old enough to be my father. I once worked for him. That's all.'

Rashad dealt her an unimpressed appraisal. 'You attended an academic dinner with him and he's a wealthy man.'

'How did you know about that dinner? He's a family friend and he needed a partner for the event. His bank balance doesn't come into it.' Her eyes were bright with the anger and resentment firing through her tense body. 'I appreciate that you really don't like me and have a very low opinion of me. So please explain—what am I doing here?'

'Look in the mirror,' Rashad advised without hesitation.

Tilda had somehow expected him to contradict her when she had accused him of not liking her. His failure to do so shook her and she could not silence the words that sprang to her lips. 'What sort of a guy wants to have a relationship with a woman he dislikes?'

'Define relationship.'

Discovering that she was suddenly super-sensitive to his every word and potential putdown, Tilda coloured to the roots of her pale hair. She got the message: his sole interest in her was physical. 'You mentioned rules,' she framed curtly, studying her tightly linked hands, telling herself that she needed to grow a thicker skin.

'No other men. I expect total fidelity.'

Tilda was so outraged by his self-assurance as it came at her like a bolt from the blue that she leapt to her feet. 'What the heck do you think I am? I've never been unfaithful to anybody!'

Rashad vented a harsh laugh of disagreement. 'I know you slept with other men while you were with me five years ago!'

Tilda blinked and then focused unbelieving turquoise eyes on his lean, vibrant face. Hauteur and fierce reserve were etched in every angular line of his startlingly handsome features. She registered in dismay that there could be no doubt that he actually believed what he was saying. 'I can hardly credit that you're accusing me of something so despicable! Why would you choose to believe something like that about me? I mean, for goodness' sake, why would I be seeing you and carrying on with other guys at the same time?'

'I was purely a business proposition.'

Her hands knotted into fists of frustration. 'So why didn't I grab you the first chance I got?'

'Playing hard to get made me keener.'

Tilda appreciated that he had long since explained any inconsistencies in her behaviour to his own satisfaction. He had made the cap fit even if it didn't belong to her. 'I did not sleep with anyone else while I was with you...what is your problem, Rashad? I was in love with you!' she launched back at him, angry with him and angry with herself for feeling cut to the bone by his demeaning misconceptions. She had found it hard enough to deal with the idea that he thought her avaricious, but to learn that he also thought she was a slut had to be the ultimate slap in the face.

'So you wanted me to believe.'

'Who are these men I'm supposed to have slept with?' she demanded furiously.

'I see no point in rehashing your past misde-meanours.' The twist of his wide, sensual mouth had more than a hint of disdain.

Undaunted, Tilda lifted her chin to a pugna-cious angle. 'Whereas I'm happy to rehash them, because the allegations you have made are com-pletely untrue!'

'I'm bored with this discussion. It's ancient history.' Rashad rested forbidding dark eyes on the animated oval of her face, wondering what she hoped to achieve with her futile protestations of innocence. 'Naturally I have seen the proof of those allegations.'

'Well, I want to see that proof!'

'That is not possible. Nor am I prepared to argue with you on this issue.'

Tilda was trembling with vexation. 'You can't confront me with accusations of that nature and then deny me the right to respond.'

His dark gaze narrowed and flashed a hard golden challenge. 'It is my belief that I can do whatever I want. If you don't like it that way, you are of course free to leave.'

Tilda was so wound up that she was on the brink of tears of fury. The dark, intimidating power of him faced her like a solid stone wall as implacable as his expression. He would not back down or compromise. His potent strength had been honed by experiences that were tougher than any she would ever know. Pinning her taut lips together, Tilda made her stiff knees bend and she lowered herself slowly back into the armchair. It was an acknowledgement of defeat that savaged her pride, but she knew that if she staged a pitched battle with him she would lose. And so, unhappily, would her family. Rashad was convinced she was a gold-digging trollop and he had evidently thought that way about her for a long time. No longer did she need to marvel at the brutality with which she had been dumped, she reflected bitterly. Whether she liked it or not, she would have to save her defence for a more promising moment. Pale as milk, and with the effort that self-discipline demanded, she folded her hands together.

'Rules,' she prompted woodenly.

'You make an effort to please me.'

Tilda dared to lift her head. 'Would you care to elaborate on that?' she pressed shakily.

'No half measures. I tell you what I want and you strive to deliver,' Rashad specified silkily. 'In where you live, in what you wear, in how you behave, in everything that you do.'

A Stepford wife without the wedding ring, Tilda thought in horror. A living, breathing puppet with a puppeteer pulling her strings at every turn. She was aghast at the prospect of Rashad taking control of her life to that extent, but not at all surprised by his expectations, for telling people what to do and how to do it came very naturally to the future King of Bakhar. Unfortunately doing as she was told when it was Rashad doing the telling did not come naturally to Tilda. While she had no problem accepting authority in other areas of her life, a rebellious demon of resentment had ignited inside her five years ago whenever Rashad had laid down the law.

'I…I thought you just wanted to sleep with me,' Tilda muttered in a small tight voice.

'Why do you have to make such a production out of it?'

'Pleasure deferred has a keener edge.' Rashad noted the fact that her thin fingers were digging convulsively into the fabric of the garment folded across her lap. She was all worked up and could not hide the fact. It did not fit his image of her and it troubled him.

Why do you have to make such a production out of it? He marvelled at that gauche comment and the implication that sex on her terms was nothing worth getting excited about. But how likely was it that so experienced a woman could also be that naïve? Most probably she was trying to manipulate him again and win his sympathy. Was anything about her real? Was her every expression and word part of an act designed to deceive? Once, she had played the innocent so well, pulling back from his passion to ensure that he lived in a torment of unslaked desire for her. That recollection roused the blazing anger and bitterness that he had kept taped down for five long years. He had wanted her as he had never wanted any woman—before or since.

'Whatever,' Tilda mumbled, loathing the level coolness of Rashad's intonation, wondering what had happened to the markedly conservative streak that had once set him apart from his much more liberal companions. No doubt, such sensitive and civilised niceties had long since bitten the dust beneath the tidal wave of uninhibited sexual licence he had been enjoying ever since he had left her. How dared he accuse her of infidelity when he had betrayed *her?* She hated him for dragging her pride in the dust. She hated him for judging her unfairly, for his determination to have the last word. She really, *really* hated him.

'On the other hand, there's no reason why you shouldn't give me a preview of what I can expect from you,' Rashad declared, the rich, dark timbre of his accented drawl smoother and softer than the most exclusive silk.

Her silvery fair head raised, jewelled eyes locking to his with instant consternation. 'A…a preview?' she parroted unevenly.

'I think you understand perfectly.'

And Tilda froze. It was a test, she was sure of it! She could not credit that he could expect her to go to bed with him there and then. Suddenly she was all for him making as much of a production of that event as he pleased. Indeed, anything that might keep that act of intimacy in the future rather than the present got her vote. Her shaken blue-green eyes tangled reluctantly with his.

His smouldering dark golden gaze was hot as a flame on her oval face. Her heart started a slow, thudding pound behind her breastbone. She was in a state of alert that left her too tense to breathe and with her tongue glued to the roof of her dry mouth. She was maddeningly aware of the heaviness of her breasts and the tingling tenderness of her nipples. Liquid heat was pooling like a rich swirl of honey in her pelvis. She shifted in her seat, suddenly unable to sit still, feeling the familiar hunger build like a dam about to break its banks and wash away her barriers.

'Come here...' Rashad urged thickly, swooping down to grasp her hand and tug her upright, impelling her straight into the proximity she would have done almost anything to avoid.

Before Tilda could even attempt to suppress her response to him, he claimed her soft, full lips with a hungry growl of resolve. The hot, hard insistence of his mouth on hers was shockingly demanding. He gave her no opportunity to deny him and the erotic plunge of his tongue into the tender interior of her mouth made her shiver violently in reaction against his big, powerful frame. Her heartbeat was racing. Every sense she possessed was reeling from the impact. The taste of him was addictive. Her hands rose to his broad shoulders initially to steady herself and then to feverishly close there. Her fingers dug into the expensive cloth of his jacket as though she needed that support to stay upright in the dizzy world of seductive sensation that enthralled her. Every kiss made her long with frantic impatience for the next. He pushed up her sweater and closed a hand on one lush full breast in a bold caress. He thrust her light cotton bra from his path and chafed a straining pink nipple.

She whimpered in shock and excitement. Her knees threatened to fold under her. There was a tight band of tension across her belly, a torment-ing feeling of need that made her push against him in blind demand for assuagement.

Rashad clamped his hands to her hips to urge her closer to the raging heat of his desire. He was as hard as iron. She wasn't resisting a single move he made. Raw triumph flooded him with all-male energy. Too well did he recall how she had once become as unresponsive as a marble statue in his arms. He bent down and scooped her off her feet at decisive speed. The sooner he sat-isfied his desire for that slim, perfect body of hers, the better. She had the morals of an alley cat. As she had said herself, making a production out of the event was most inappropriate. For what reason would he wait?

Tilda gasped for air to ease her oxygen-starved lungs. Trembling like a leaf in a high wind, she opened anxious eyes to focus on Rashad's lean darkly handsome face above hers. He had snatched her up into his powerful arms as though

she weighed no more than a doll. 'Where are we
g-going?' she stammered.

Rashad kicked open a door with controlled
force. He had appointments to keep, not to
mention a flight to New York scheduled. He
didn't care. Just for once in his life he was going
to do what he wanted to do, not what he *should*
do! He wanted her now; he did not want to wait
one hour longer. Had he not waited five years
already? He settled her down on his bed and immediately undid the clip that confined her hair.
He sank caressing hands into the tumbling mass
and drew it across her slight shoulders so that it
fell almost to her waist in a glorious snaking
tangle of platinum-blond ringlets.

Aghast to find herself on a bed when mere
minutes earlier she had been safe in a drawing
room, Tilda stared up at him wide-eyed. The
Rashad she remembered would never have
kissed her like that and swept her off into a
bedroom without hesitation. He had treated her
with respect and restraint. She was stunned by
the change in him. Even briefly deprived of his

caresses her body leapt and tingled with a sensual aftershock so powerful that it almost hurt not to drag him down to her again. 'Rashad…'

Rashad unbuttoned his jacket with a masculine air of purpose. Scorching golden eyes assailed hers with fierce intensity. 'Here in my bed we will seal our new understanding.'

'Now?' Tilda was appalled by that declaration of intent. She would not let herself think about how her enthusiastic response to his passion could only have encouraged him to believe that it was fine to regard her as a midmorning sexual snack. 'I mean, right here and now?'

Rashad surveyed her with compelling force. 'It is my wish.'

He was dangerously accustomed to instant acquiescence with his expressed wishes and immediate gratification, Tilda acknowledged in a daze. She was already battling to come to terms with the idea of willingly becoming Rashad's plaything, his possession, his little toy. Suddenly the sheer weight of such expectations was too much for her to handle at that moment.

'I can't!' she gasped. 'Not right now anyhow.'

Rashad had not considered that possibility. A lean brown hand clenched in frustration and then loosened again for the depth of his reserve had made the concealment of his every private reaction instinctive. The ache of sexual arousal was so sharp and frustrating that it felt like a physical pain. 'Then we must wait until you reach Bakhar.'

Tilda flushed to her hairline when she realised the meaning he had mistakenly taken from her outburst. She lowered her head, knowing she was not about to correct him and wondering if that made her a terrible cheat. Like one of those women who famously feigned continual headaches? But before she could let her thoughts stray in that direction, all of what he had just said finally sank in and she raised shaken turquoise eyes. 'You're planning to take me back to Bakhar with you?'

'I have a palace in the desert. The harem is tailor-made for a woman like you.' Rashad was thinking with savage satisfaction of Tilda in the Palace of the Lions, isolated by the remote location from the temptations of the rest of the world and forced to depend only on him for company and amusement. That would soon sort her out. She would be his very personal project. There would be no more lies, no more deceits and no more pretence.

Outraged and convinced he was joking in a very unfunny way, Tilda slid off the bed and hurriedly sidestepped him while trying not to look as if she was running away. She paused by the door. 'I know you've got to be teasing me. You once told me that there was no such thing as a harem anywhere in Bakhar.'

Rashad gave her a sardonic appraisal, enjoying her disbelief and the hint of panic she couldn't hide. It was but a small repayment for the sexual disappointment she had just dealt him. *Again*. She had had no business giving him such encouragement when she could not offer him release. But hadn't that been typical of her? To yield just a provocative taste of her exquisite body to tantalise and tease him?

'I mean, I know you're too civilised to try and treat me like a concubine…or something,'

Tilda proffered in a small, tight voice of deep audible suspicion.

'My grandfather had hundreds of concubines. We don't talk about it. It's not politically correct these days. But the royal household always had concubines. Most of them were gifts from their families. It was considered an honour to enter the royal harem and a good way of gaining the favour of the ruling family,' Rashad confided lazily, watching her gorgeous eyes widen and her ripe lower lip part from the upper in disquiet. 'Alas, I will have to satisfy myself with only you, but think of all the attention you'll get. At least you won't have to compete with other women or share me.'

'I'm not going to be anybody's concubine, especially not yours!' Tilda shot at him vehemently, yanking open the door and hastening out into the corridor.

Rashad, who had never thought of himself as an imaginative man, pictured Tilda reclining in something very flimsy on a bed in the Palace of the Lions, counting the days and the hours until he would visit her there. He found that vivid mental image so deeply attractive that it was an effort to move on from it to consider more practical aspects. When had anyone last lived at the old palace? He would have to throw an army of servants into the ancient building and refurbish it from roof to basement for occupation. It would be a huge task. His staff would be kept extremely busy.

'How long are you expecting me to stay in Bakhar for?'

'For as long as I want you in my bed.' Rashad thrust open the drawing-room door.

Tilda swallowed painfully. 'If I agree—'

'You've already agreed.'

'You have to write off the loan and sign the house back to Mum.'

His colourful reverie most effectively dispersed by that evidence of her financial acuteness, Rashad surveyed her with hard dark eyes. 'You think you'll be worth that much money?'

Tilda promised herself that somehow, some day, some way, she would get revenge for what he was doing to her. Pale as death, she knotted her restive hands together and veiled her angry, mortified gaze. 'It's what you think that matters,' she pointed out flatly. 'But if you want me to hand myself over body and soul and put my whole life on hold for goodness knows how long, I need to know that my family's going to be all right while I'm away.'

'There speaks the martyr,' Rashad murmured with scorn.

Tilda would not allow herself to react to that inflammatory comment. 'When will you stop the eviction proceedings?'

'The day you fly into Bakhar. That will give you ten days at most to get organised.'

Tilda dealt him a stricken look of condemnation. 'You can't do it that way!'

'I don't trust you, so the pressure stays on. There will be no room for renegotiating in the hope of more favourable and lucrative terms and no opportunity for you to renege on the deal.' Having glanced out the window and noted the expensive Jaguar awaiting her return, Rashad turned his arrogant dark head to study her with chilling intensity. 'In the meantime, you should be careful to be on your very best behaviour.'

'Best behaviour?' Her brow furrowed. 'What are you talking about?'

'Your lover has come back to pick you up. But you can't get into his car again, or be alone with him or any other man now. I'm a very suspicious guy and I will have you watched from the moment you leave this house until you reach Bakhar. If there is so much as a hint of flirtation or questionable behaviour, the deal is off and the eviction proceedings will go ahead.'

Tilda stared back at him in mute incredulity and horror. 'You're threatening me.'

'I am warning you that if you disappoint me you will suffer punitive consequences. Get rid of your elderly chauffeur now. The clock is already ticking,' Rashad murmured with lethal cool.

Tilda dug into her bag for her mobile phone and rang Evan in haste. She told him that it would be quite some time until she was free to leave and that there was absolutely no point in him waiting for her.

'Excellent. I was always convinced that with the correct approach you would find it very easy to follow instructions,' Rashad drawled lazily.

Tilda quivered with rage and frustration. She felt as if a tornado were locked inside her and fighting for exit. But she dared not explode; she dared not offend or antagonise him because he had the power to rip her family apart. She wanted to tell him how much she hated him. Instead, loathing seethed inside her and she had to hold it in.

Someone knocked on the door and entered to address Rashad in his own language.

'I have to leave for the airport,' Rashad imparted. 'I will have you conveyed home. I'll be in touch with further directions.'

Her silvery fair head lifted, turquoise eyes burning brilliant blue. 'Yes, Your Royal Highness. Anything else?'

'I'll be sure to let you know.' Emanating a positive force field of masculine power and authority and untouched by her silent hostility, Rashad sent her a shuttered glance of cool, calm satisfaction.

From the drawing-room window above, Tilda watched him climb into his big black limo. Ten minutes later she got into the Mercedes that had been ordered to take her home. All she would let herself think about was the story she would tell her family. She practised a breezy smile and a cheerful voice. Her surrender on Rashad's terms would be totally wasted if her mother suspected even a hint of the unlovely truth.

'I've got fantastic news. Rashad has just offered me a terrific job,' she told Beth Morrison when she got home again. 'It will pay well enough to eventually clear all the money that we owe.'

The older woman was initially astonished, but her palpable relief soon silenced her surprised questions. 'Of course! You came first on your accountancy course, so Rashad will be getting a top-notch employee. I'm so glad I wasn't wrong about him. I always thought Rashad was a decent and trustworthy young man,' Beth contended happily. 'Where will you be working?'

'Bakhar.'

'Oh, my goodness, this new job will be abroad! I should've thought of that possibility,' her mother exclaimed. 'We'll all miss you so much. Are you sure this is the right thing for you?'

'Oh, totally.' Tilda kept right on smiling although her jaw was beginning to ache.

Her supposed new career move was the sole topic of discussion amongst her siblings that evening. As none of them was aware of the severity of the family financial problems, the assumption was that Tilda had won her dream job. 'I suppose working abroad will be a nice change for you,' Aubrey, her brother, commented vaguely before he went back upstairs to swot. A year her junior, he was exceptionally clever and, like many intellectual people, quite removed from the practicalities of life.

Her teenaged brother, James, gave her an impressed look. 'You can earn a fortune tax-free in the Middle East!'

'Will you go to work on a camel every morning?' her little sister, Megan, asked hopefully.

Her other sister, Katie, was more thoughtful and less easily convinced by the surface show of normality. As the sisters got ready for bed in the room they shared, the teenager's blue eyes were troubled. 'What was it like for you seeing Rashad again? Didn't you just hate him?'

'No, I got over all that a long time ago,' Tilda whispered, not wanting to waken Megan.

'But you've never really gone out with anyone since him.'

Turning her head to the wall, Tilda shut her eyes tight. 'That's nothing to do with Rashad. I mean, relationships aren't for everyone,' she muttered. 'I've had a few dates—they just haven't led anywhere.'

'Because you're not interested…the guys always are—'

'I haven't got time for a man.'

'You had time for Rashad when he was around.'

Stinging tears foamed up behind Tilda's lowered lids. She swallowed back the ache in her throat and told herself not to be so foolish. She then lay awake for half of the night fretting about how her family would manage a hundred and one different tasks without her help. She was also aware that she had to sort out Scott. Those twin concerns screened out the even bigger worry about how she would handle Rashad. The next morning she handed in her notice at work and when she had finished for the day she caught the bus to her stepfather's house.

'What do you want?' Scott demanded menacingly on the doorstep.

'If you ever try to take money from my mother again, I'll report you to the police,' Tilda told him. 'If you threaten or hurt any member of my family, I'll also go straight to the police, so leave us alone!'

The furious resentment with which the older man hurled a tide of abuse at her convinced her that her warning would scare him off. Like most bullies, Scott usually avoided people who fought back and concentrated his aggression on milder personalities.

She was waiting for another bus when her mobile phone went off.

'I thought your stepfather was history,'

Rashad's voice remarked with crystal clarity in her ear.

Surprise almost made Tilda jump a foot in the air. 'I thought you were in New York!'

'I am.'

'So how do you know I'd been at my stepfather's house?'

'My security staff are superb at surveillance. I told you I would watch over you,' Rashad drawled lazily. 'Why were you visiting Morrison?'

Tilda cast a harried and cross glance up and down the street, which was as busy as most residential areas were at that time of the evening. But there was no sign of anyone paying her particular attention; if there had been she was in the right mood to give them a piece of her mind. 'None of your business. I can't imagine why you're taking the trouble to put Nosy Parkers on my trail!'

'Nothing is too much trouble when it comes to my favourite concubine.' An unholy grin of amusement slowly curving his handsome mouth and putting his formidable cool reserve to flight,

Rashad relaxed his lean, powerful body back into his office chair and listened to the line being cut with a furious click. There was a powerful buzz to his every exchange or encounter with Tilda. That truth disturbed him...

CHAPTER FIVE

THE car door of the Mercedes opened. The chauffeur bowed low and the bodyguards fanned out. Her heart beating very fast, Tilda climbed out and walked into the hotel, striving to appear indifferent to all the heads turning to look in her direction. The lift was held for her benefit. Moments later, she was ushered into an opulent suite and shown straight into a bedroom where a complete change of clothes awaited her.

Her palms were damp as she unbuttoned the jacket of the ordinary navy trouser suit she had worn. She undressed with great care. Leaving home had upset her and keeping up the cheerful front had been a challenge. It was her second visit to this London hotel. Her first had taken place over a week earlier, when a couple of

hours had passed while she had been compre-
hensively measured for a new wardrobe. Both
trips had been organised by an anonymous voice
over the phone. She'd had to put on pressure to
find out exactly when she would be flying out
to Bakhar. From Rashad himself, she had heard
not a word. While she was by no means keen for
any unnecessary contact with him, that silence
had done nothing to lessen her apprehensions
about her future.

Tilda donned the cobweb-fine silk and lace
lingerie. Each item was a perfect fit. She had
never known anyone who wore stockings. She
liked her underwear plain and comfortable, not
designed to present the female body in a provocative way. The gossamer-thin bra and briefs
offered nothing in the way of concealment. In
spite of the warmth of the room she shivered.
She slid into the beautifully made blue dress and
eased her feet into the delicate high-heeled
shoes. She was reaching for the matching light
coat when the very expensive mobile phone
lying on the bed rang.

After a moment of hesitation, she answered it. 'Hello?'

'Leave your hair loose,' Rashad murmured huskily.

It was an effort to find her voice. 'Right.'

'The phone is yours. It enjoys enhanced security. Wear the jewellery. I'm looking forward to seeing you at the airport.' Rashad rang off.

Moving with as much enthusiasm as an automaton, Tilda tucked the fancy phone into the designer handbag on the bed. A jewel box reposed on the dressing table. She flipped it open, anxious eyes widening at the sight of the dazzling platinum and diamond set pendant and drop earrings. Her hands all thumbs, she put the jewellery on. She unclasped her hair and reached for a comb. He had always loved her hair. A tremor ran through her slender length. At that instant she was tempted to hack her hair off to within a few inches of her scalp.

But how would her desert prince react? Suppose that hair was her main attraction in his eyes? Suppose he took one look at her shorn of her crowning glory and rejected her at the airport? It was not a risk she could afford to take. Her lovely face tightening, she tidied her hair and slid into the light coat. Her reflection in the mirror mocked her, for the conservative outfit adorned with the eye-catching jewellery was very stylish. On the surface she looked like a lady, she conceded bitterly, but both she and, more importantly, *he* knew that beneath the elegant restraint of her outer garments she was dressed like his favourite concubine.

She travelled to Heathrow in an enormous limousine embellished with tinted windows. She was walking through the airport terminal when someone called her name. She came to a surprised halt and turned her head and was instantly targeted by a blinding onslaught of flashing cameras borne by running people. In the commotion questions were shouted at her while the security team accompanying her banded round her in a protective huddle and urged her on.

'How does it feel to be the Crown Prince's latest lady?'

'Turn this way, luv…let us get a shot of the sparklers round your neck!'

'Are you flying out to meet the Bakhari royal family?' A woman yelled, trotting alongside her and extending a microphone. 'Is it true you first met when Prince Rashad was up at Oxford?'

Aghast at the attention and the intrusive interrogation, Tilda sped on almost at a run and kept her head bent down to discourage further photos being taken. Another couple of bodyguards came rushing up in support of their beleaguered colleagues and hastily ushered her out of the main concourse, down a corridor and into a private room.

Her dismayed eyes collided without warning with Rashad's searing golden scrutiny. Although the austere classic lines of his lean, strong face bore his customary air of detachment, Tilda felt as jolted as if she had stuck her finger into a live electric socket: wrath emanated from him in a force field. He inclined his arrogant dark head in a clear signal for her to approach him. She would have preferred to stay where she was. On the other hand she did not want to run the risk of being ordered around in front of his staff, all of whom were clumped in a corner being careful to neither speak nor look in their direction.

'I will deal with this matter after we board.' Rashad's low-pitched intonation somehow achieved the same stinging effect as the flick of a whip.

Tilda's sense of intimidation was put to flight by a surge of annoyance. Here she was packaged and presented from head to toe and from the skin out as His Royal Highness had commanded. She had done exactly as she had been told. She had not put a foot wrong. What was the matter with him? Was he never satisfied? Her life promised to be hell for the duration of their relationship, she thought angrily. But she was quick to remind herself that the reward was that, within twenty-four hours, all immediate threat to the stability of her family would be eradicated.

She stole a grudging glance at Rashad from below her honey-brown lashes and her tummy flipped with an immediacy that infuriated her. He was breathtakingly handsome. Yet there was something more compelling than mere good looks in his lean, sculpted features, something that ensnared her and made her want to look again and again. Five years earlier, she had been hopelessly addicted to him and wildly in love. A deep pang of pain assailed her at that recollection and chilled her to the marrow. No, she promised herself staunchly, never again would she allow her more tender emotions to overwhelm her in Rashad's radius. She could not afford to make herself that vulnerable again.

His private jet was large and the interior so sumptuous it took Tilda's breath away. She sank into an extremely comfortable seat and braced herself for take-off while ruminating over what might have annoyed him. Was it the startling interest that the press had demonstrated in her at the airport? Well, that was scarcely her fault. He was a fabulously wealthy womaniser and royal into the bargain. The paparazzi adored him and tracked his movements round the globe. His social life filled gossip-page columns every month and occasionally even attracted headlines.

Soon after the plane had left the runway, Rashad undid his seat belt and rose from his seat with swift movements. 'You may now answer my questions.'

Tilda, who had only flown a couple of times in her entire life, relaxed her white-knuckled grip on the arms of her seat and opened her eyes. 'What is wrong?' she asked, shaking her pale blond head in bewilderment. 'I've done nothing and I already feel like I'm on trial.'

Rashad surveyed her with lustrous dark eyes of suspicion. He could not recall when he had last come so close to losing his temper. Her luminous turquoise eyes rested on him in seemingly innocent enquiry. But the very fact that she had contrived to home in on his one oversight and take advantage of it convinced him that once again she was acting.

'Why did you tip off the press about our travel plans?'

Tilda blinked, letting the ramifications of that far-reaching question sink in. Outrage flashed through her. 'Now just you listen here,' she gasped, struggling to undo her seat belt with furious hands.

Rashad crouched down on a level with her. 'No, you listen,' he urged soft and low and deadly in warning. 'If you shout, you will be overheard and you will embarrass my staff. Impertinence and discourtesy are much disliked in Bakhar.'

Fit to be tied, Tilda trembled with rage and chagrin. 'You're the only person who makes me feel like this—'

Rashad undid the seat belt that had defeated her with a deft flick of one hand and subjected her to the full assault of his stunning dark golden eyes. 'You are strong-willed. I'm the only person who stands up to you.'

Tilda scrambled up and took herself over to the other side of the cabin. Her oval face flushed, she spun round again before he could remind her that it was rude to turn her back on him. 'You're also the only person who continually makes me the target of unjust accusations. Surely that is some excuse for a loss of temper?' she whispered back at him vehemently, her hands balled into fists of restraint by her side. 'I've never had any contact with the press. I haven't a clue about how to go about tipping them off, either.'

Rashad dealt her a sizzling appraisal. 'I cannot accept that. Five years ago the paparazzi barely knew of my existence and my association with you was never revealed in print. But today, even though I have never yet appeared in public with you, the paparazzi were waiting for your arrival. They have already identified you and made reference to our past acquaintance. Who else could have whetted their appetite with such details?'

'How would I know? It wasn't me!' Tilda protested.

'Sooner or later, you will have to tell me the truth,' Rashad delivered with hard resolve. 'Lies are at all times unacceptable to me.'

Tilda ground her teeth together. 'I'm not lying to you. Why would I tip off the press? Do you think I'm proud of the reason why I'm allowing myself to be flown out to your country?'

'*Enough,*' Rashad shot at her in a warning growl, marvelling at her ability to stand there looking so exquisitely beautiful while she went for him like a spitting, clawing tigress. But he meant every word that he had spoken. He would not settle for lies. She had strength and intelligence. He was convinced that if he was tough enough with her, those virtues would rise nearer the surface.

Tilda picked a seat as far away from him as she could. Silence fell, and it was a silence laden with angry tension. A sun of impotent rage was rising inside her. According to *him*, everything that went wrong was her fault and now she couldn't even shout at him. Where was the justice in that? How dared he blame her for the level of press interest in his fast-lane life with models and actresses? From where did he get the brass neck to continually take the moral high ground? In comparison she lived a life of unblemished virtue. So, she wasn't perfect? So what! Was he?

Temper still simmering, Tilda shot him a furious glance. 'Do you really think that I have any wish to be publicly known as your trollop?'

Rashad had to dig deep into his reserves to maintain silence in the face of such unbridled provocation. His *trollop*? He set his perfect white teeth together and flexed long, shapely brown fingers. Once the jet landed, his staff reappeared to disembark and Rashad was approached by his current senior aide, Butrus. A professor of law and an excellent administrator, the older man made a rather strained enquiry as to what designation he should place on Tilda's visa to enter Bakhar.

Rashad's anger, all the more powerful for being denied utterance, was still intense. Wrathfully impatient of the bureaucracy of petty detail that the royal family had always been exempt from, Rashad responded in his own language and with an unashamed resolution that none would dare to question. 'She is my woman. She does not require a visa.'

Butrus froze, then went straight into retreat and bowed very low. An electric silence enveloped them all, his entire staff falling still. An almost imperceptible hint of colour demarcating his high cheekbones, Rashad realised that for the first time in his life he had shown his stormy emotions in public. As quickly, he decided that his candour might have shocked but it had not been a mistake. He closed a fierce hand over Tilda's pale, delicate fingers. He could not possibly keep her a secret from those closest to him and, although he had not planned to make such a dramatic announcement, at least, he reasoned, nobody was now in any doubt about her non-negotiable status in his life.

'You're hurting my hand,' Tilda stretched up on tiptoe to snap.

Rashad immediately loosened his possessive hold, but he did not let her go. She was his now, he thought with satisfaction. She was in Bakhar with him. He smoothed her crushed digits between a caressing forefinger and thumb and retained her hand in his. Taken aback by that response to her waspish complaint, Tilda looked up at him. A slow-burning smile slashed his beautiful mouth. Engulfed in that unexpected warmth, she felt dizzy and breathless.

Across the cabin, Butrus watched that visual exchange of smiles in sincere wonderment before hastily averting his attention from the display. All of a sudden he finally understood why the Palace of the Lions was being prepared for occupation and he was appalled by his mis-interpretation of his royal employer's meaning. How could he have been so foolish as to credit that the Crown Prince might defy the conven-tions to the extent of importing a foreign mistress? Instead, Prince Rashad had taken a re-freshingly traditional path to matrimony, which would bring great joy to his family and the entire country of Bakhar. A marriage by declaration. Was it not truly typical of their heroic and fiercely independent prince that he should choose a bride and bring her home without any of the usual fuss? As soon as his employer had left the plane, Butrus got on the phone to break the happy tidings to King Hazar's closest advisor, Jasim, and ensure that scandalous rumours could gain no ground whatsoever in the royal household. He was little disappointed by the discovery that the happy tidings were not quite the surprise he had envisaged.

Tilda was quite unprepared for the roasting heat of Bakhar midafternoon and briefly forgot that she was demonstrating her supreme disdain for Rashad by not speaking to him. 'Is it always this hot?'

Even this faintest hint of criticism of the Bakhari climate made Rashad square his broad shoulders. 'It is a beautiful day. There are no gloomy grey skies here in early summer.'

An air-conditioned limo pulled up and whisked them past a very large new airport terminal. The vehicle carried them only a couple of hundred yards before setting them down again beside a large white-and-gold helicopter. Boarding, she sat down on a fitted cream sofa and tried not to gape at the space and comfort surrounding her.

The panoramic view soon stole her attention. The helicopter followed a craggy line of mountains and flew over green fertile valleys before reaching the desert interior. Her first glimpse of the great ochre-coloured sand dunes rolling towards the horizon enthralled her. Far below she saw a camel train trekking out into the great emptiness and, once or twice, encampments of black tents. Children chased the shadow of the helicopter and waved frantically, and still the desert stretched like a vast, endless golden ocean ahead of them.

'How much farther?' she was finally moved to ask.

'Another ten minutes or so.' Rashad had instructed the pilot to give them a scenic grand tour and the flight had been much longer than necessary. Although he usually found a fresh sight of the country he loved an energising experience, he had barely removed his keen dark gaze from Tilda's delicate, feminine profile. His hunger to possess her was stabbing at him like a knife.

He had watched while she knelt laughing on the seat and waved back at the Bedouin children with youthful enthusiasm. *Joie de vivre,* the French called it, and that sparkling quality of joy had once had enormous appeal for a male who had grown from a solemn little boy into a very serious young man. The emotion Tilda showed so freely had been a powerful source of attraction. Exasperation made him suppress those memories. The present, he told himself bleakly, was more relevant. Yes, she was very desirable. But had he not bought her into his bed? Where was the appeal in that? Or in her lies?

Picking up on the dry note in his rich dark drawl, Tilda went pink. She smoothed down her dress and sat down in a more circumspect fashion. 'Will I be able to shout at you when we arrive wherever we're going?'

'No. I tell you what I want and you strive to deliver,' Rashad reminded her with immense cool.

A little quiver of nervous tension rippled through Tilda for there was a shimmering golden light in his gaze. 'What if I disappoint you?'

'You won't.'

Tilda sucked in a stark breath.

'I think you'll learn fast,' Rashad murmured lazily.

Her face burning, Tilda turned her head away and saw an immense building perched on the rocky hillside directly ahead. The helicopter swooped in over the outer walls and landed. She stepped out into the fresh air, her fascinated eyes climbing the weathered battlements of the ancient gate tower ahead.

'Welcome to the Palace of the Lions,' Rashad intoned, feeling the pulse of his mobile phone as it sought his attention. He tensed and then reached into his pocket to switch it off. He had always taken his duties very seriously, and it was an act that cost him a tussle with his conscience, but he was determined not to be distracted from Tilda. For just a few precious hours he would forget his royal responsibilities.

Beyond the tower lay a yet more imposing entrance dominated by very tall carved doors. 'It's an incredibly old building,' Tilda remarked, struggling not to be intimidated. 'Is this where you live?'

'It belongs to me but I have only stayed here occasionally. One of my ancestors built the palace. When our people were nomads this was the seat of power in Bakhar. My grandfather died, our main city grew in size and this building gradually fell into disuse.'

They passed into a vast echoing entrance hall. Light flickered and danced over the glinting reflective surfaces of the tiny coloured mirror tiles set into the intricately patterned ceiling. Tilda glanced through doorways and saw tantalising glimpses of rooms furnished in a highly exotic mix of Victorian and middle-eastern décor that dated back at least a century in style. The palace appeared to be well and truly stuck in a time warp.

'My goodness,' Tilda remarked helplessly. 'It's like walking into a time capsule.'

Rashad tensed. Presented with an enormous challenge and a tiny timeframe his staff had done their best, but had felt forced to concentrate on matters such as the plumbing, the electrical fixtures and the lack of air-conditioning.

'Totally fascinating,' she confided, craning her neck to admire an ancient hanging on the wall depicting a robed horseman waving a sword in the bloodthirsty heat of battle.

A servant appeared and fell to his knees in front of Rashad. He broke into a flood of apology, for Rashad had given a command that under no circumstances was he to be disturbed. The man laid a phone at his royal employer's feet with an air of entreaty.

Rashad compressed his handsome mouth and repeated his instruction. A hundred and one matters, and a hundred and one people at court, in government and from abroad, demanded his attention every day—and he never, ever took a day off. But this particular day was different: he was with Tilda. Obviously he had not been firm enough in his command. He stepped over the phone.

'Is there a problem?' Tilda enquired, peering back at the hapless older man literally wringing his hands and muttering laments. 'He seems a bit upset.'

'Drama is the spice of life to my people.'

Angling her bright gaze back to Rashad, Tilda lifted her chin and finally said what had been simmering at the back of her mind for hours. 'I didn't tip off the press and I can't imagine why you think I would've done.'

'Many women revel in that sort of public attention. There are also those who choose to make money by selling personal information to the paparazzi.'

That inflammatory comeback tensed her narrow spine into rigidity and she decided to give him the response he deserved. She spun round, platinum-fair curls falling in silvery streamers round her exquisite face, her jewelled eyes hurling a challenge. 'Actually I don't plan to sell my story of what it's like to be a prince's concubine until I go home again.'

The atmosphere sizzled like oil heated to boiling point.

Dense black lashes sweeping low on his scorching golden gaze, Rashad strolled silently back to her, intrigued by her continuing defiance. 'Perhaps,' he murmured very softly, 'you won't want to go home again. I can be very persuasive.'

Tilda had wanted to annoy him and the tenor of his reply took her by surprise. 'Of course I'll want to go home again…I'll be counting the days!'

'Or you'll be doing whatever it takes to hold my interest so that you can stay. Today you stop running away and start learning.' A lean brown hand lifted to brush a straying strand of pale hair back from her cheekbone in a confident gesture of intimacy. She backed up against the cold solid wall, her breath catching in her throat. He traced the pouting cupid's bow of her upper lip with his thumb and gently opened her mouth to graze the soft moist underside. Her legs went limp and stinging awareness made her nipples pinch into painfully tight buds. It was a fight to contain the wanton shock of fascination travelling through her.

'I don't run away,' she told him frantically. *'Ever!'*

'Once, you ran faster than a gazelle every time I got too close. I'm a hunter. I enjoyed the chase.' Rashad let his forefinger dip sexily between her peach-soft lips and retreat again. He watched her pupils dilate and the slender white expanse of her throat extend as she tipped her head back in instinctive female invitation. 'But you always wanted me. You may fight with me, but you are begging for my mouth right now.'

Her long brown lashes fluttered. It took enormous effort to concentrate again. Angry pain slashed through that mental fog because for a long, timeless moment she had craved the heat of his mouth on hers as badly as a life-giving drug. 'I'm not begging,' she muttered, forcing a laugh that sounded horribly strangled.

Rashad gazed down at her with a languorous heat that made her tremble. 'Don't worry—you will.'

Tilda braced a hand on the wall and pushed herself away from him with a lack of coordination that infuriated her. She was trembling, maddeningly aware of every fluid shift of his lithe, powerful body so close to hers. Her mind threw up a dangerous image of Rashad pushing her back against the wall with the passion that was so much a part of him, the passion he so rarely freed from restraint. The knot of tension in her pelvis tightened and she recognised it for the hunger it was. The fact that her hostility didn't stop her responding to him shook her up badly.

Rashad shot her pale, taut profile a glittering appraisal and closed a shapely brown hand over hers. 'Let me show you the harem.'

'I can hardly wait.' Although colour now mantled her cheeks, Tilda lifted her head high. She remembered his dark sense of humour so well. She remembered how he had once teased the life out of her. A sharp pang of regret gripped her for that lost time and had the effect of simply hardening her resolve.

'I didn't tip off the press,' she told him afresh.

'So you say.' His audible indifference to such a plea incensed her.

'And five years ago, I didn't sleep with anyone else.'

Rashad expelled his breath in a long-suffering hiss. Why did she keep on reminding him of her infidelity? He did not want to be reminded. Why did she not appreciate that every denial merely acted as a prompt to unsavoury memories?

Mounting a vast stone staircase by his side and determined to ignore the discouraging silence that had met her valiant claim, Tilda swallowed hard. 'I'd like to see the proof you said you had of my so-called misdemeanours.'

'Some day I will let you see it.' Rashad flashed her an impatient look. As she could have no idea how conclusive his proof was she was probably hoping to argue her way out of the evidence of her deceit. Unhappily for her, he had complete faith in the source of the information he had received.

'Why not now?'

'I have heard enough of your lies. Silence is preferable.' His lean, darkly handsome face was resolute. 'In time, I expect you to accept the futility of lying to me.'

Tilda yanked her hand forcibly free of his. 'So you intend to make it impossible for me to defend myself. I'm damned if I do speak up and damned if I don't. But why would any man want a lying, cheating gold-digger?'

Rashad made no answer. He refused to rise to the bait. He was beginning to appreciate that whenever she was most desperate to keep him at a distance she started fighting with him.

Aggrieved by his lack of response, Tilda murmured dulcetly, 'Maybe you only like bad girls.'

At that crack, Rashad surveyed her with pure predatory appreciation. Where she was concerned that was true. When he looked at her, when he thought about her, her sins were never at the forefront of his mind. His desire ran too hot and strong to be denied. With her turquoise eyes as vivid as polar stars, she glowed with beauty and quicksilver energy. The ache at his groin came close to pain. Never had he felt such powerful need to possess a woman. Suddenly all his patience just vanished. He strode forward and swept her up off her feet and headed for his bedroom.

'What the heck are you doing?' Tilda launched at him in astonishment.

'We've waited long enough to be together.' Rashad thrust at a door with a broad shoulder to force it wider and kicked it shut in his wake.

Tilda spread a decidedly panicky glance round the echoing bedroom, which seemed to her to have very little else in it beyond the highly ornate four-poster bed that sat on a dais. 'I thought I was going to get a tour of the harem!'

'Some other day, when I have the strength to resist you.' Rashad lowered her to the floor and stripped off her coat, an imprisoning hand splaying across the soft swell of her hips in case she dared to stray anywhere out of his reach. He bent his arrogant dark head, golden eyes smouldering over her like tiny flames, and tasted her soft full mouth.

It was as though every time he touched her he sent another brick flying out of her wall of defence, leaving her more at risk and less able to hold out against him the next time. His insistent kiss jolted her like a bolt of lightning shooting down her spine and made her go back for more. Her heart raced and her body quivered against the hard, masculine promise of his. He pried her lips apart for the erotic plunge of his tongue. Her tummy flipped with sheer excitement. She could not withstand her need to touch him. Her hands slid beneath his jacket to trace the warm, hard contours of his powerful chest beneath the fine shirt.

Rashad raised his head, luxuriant ebony lashes lifting to frame golden eyes alight with hunger. He eased her dress off her narrow shoulders and let it slide down to her feet in a heap. She was startled, for she had not realised that he had already unzipped the garment. Suddenly feeling very exposed in her flimsy bra and briefs, she wrapped her arms round herself.

'Don't embarrass me by acting as though you are shy,' Rashad derided, long brown fingers enclosing her wrists to uncross her arms again. Such pretence from her hit the rawest of nerves and his annoyance with her was intense. 'I hate anything false. Fake modesty leaves me cold. Why would I even want you to be a virgin?'

Tilda jerked back from him in a defensive movement. *Why would I even want you to be a virgin?* That scornful demand faded the pink from her cheeks. He recognised the hollow light in her clear eyes and, disturbed by that awareness, he reached for her again, determined to break through her resistance.

'Did you think that pretence is what I want from you?' Rashad demanded in a roughened undertone. 'It was not my intention to cause you pain. But this time I want only what is real from you.'

Tilda was shaken that he had noticed that he had hurt her feelings, because she had believed she was better at hiding her feelings. He framed her face with his lean hands and took her mouth with ravishing sweetness and spellbinding sensuality. She stopped thinking and let her response take over. He curved her slender, unresisting body to his, drinking in the scent of her creamy white skin and the telling unsteadiness of her breathing. Lifting her onto the bed, he stood back to discard his tie and unbutton his shirt.

Her limbs felt heavy where they lay on the crimson silk spread and there was a liquid heat burning low in her belly. She could not take her eyes off the light golden slice of male torso he had revealed: muscle rippled across the solid wall of his chest as he took off the shirt, and black whorls of hair dusted his pectorals and arrowed down in a silken furrow across the flat slab of his stomach. Her mouth ran dry.

Rashad surveyed her with smouldering appreciation and the mattress gave under his weight. Tilda rolled away. Rashad laughed and hauled her back to him with easy strength. 'You are so beautiful,' he told her thickly, tasting her luscious mouth again, dipping his tongue between her parted lips with a dark sensuality that left her trembling. 'You want me, too.'

She shut her eyes for fear that he could read that truth there. The tiny moments when he wasn't touching her were already a torment. Like a doll, she was incapable of independent action and it was the very strength of her desire for him that kept her trapped. He pressed his hard, sensual mouth against the tiny pulse going crazy below her collar-bone and she gasped and arched her narrow spine. He pulled her back against him to unclasp her bra. A groan of male satisfaction sounded in his throat when her small, high breasts tumbled free. He teased the swollen pink peaks with skilful fingers, before he bent over her and used his mouth to toy with the straining buds. Every bitter-sweet sensation darted straight as an arrow to the hot damp pulse between her thighs and increased the ache there.

'Rashad…oh, please…'

Rashad looked down at her with heavily lidded eyes, lashes so long they almost hit his superb cheekbones. Somewhere outside he heard the sharp crack of rifles releasing a hail of bullets and he frowned.

'What's that?' she mumbled breathlessly, her fingers delving into the luxuriant depths of his black hair.

'Someone has probably got married and the guards are showing their appreciation.' Although that was the most likely explanation, Rashad was tense as only a former soldier could be in such circumstances. Then he heard the drone of aircraft. As he leapt off the bed and snatched up his shirt a jet flew overhead. Barely twenty seconds later, he heard the heavy whop-whop of more than one helicopter approaching.

'Rashad? What's happening?' Tilda prompted apprehensively.

'Get dressed.' An urgent knocking sounded on the door. The noise was almost drowned out by the ear-splitting whine of another jet flashing over the palace.

Rashad answered the door.

'Please forgive the intrusion, Your Royal Highness,' a senior manservant delivered anxiously, 'but I have been asked to inform you that the Prime Minister is about to arrive. He most humbly requests an audience with you.'

Every scrap of colour in Rashad's lean, strong face ebbed. He turned the colour of burnt ashes, because he could only think that something had happened to his father. For what other reason would the Prime Minister come to see him without having organised the visit in advance?

'Rashad?' Tilda pressed worriedly.

Rashad looked through her as if she had suddenly become invisible. At speed he donned his tie and jacket. 'Do not on any account leave this room, or speak to anyone, until I return.'

CHAPTER SIX

RASHAD had only got as far as the landing when he recalled his mobile phone, which he had switched off, and he immediately put it on again. He cursed the selfish streak of recklessness that had caused him to ignore the phone's demands barely thirty minutes earlier. Almost immediately, the ringtone sounded again and he answered it. Informed that his royal parent was waiting to speak to him, he was bewildered.

'My son,' King Hazar boomed on the line as if he were addressing a packed audience chamber, 'I am overjoyed!'

'You are in good health, my father?' Rashad breathed in astonishment.

'Of course.'

Rashad was still shaken by the fear that had

seized him. 'Then, why has the Prime Minister flown out to the desert to speak to me?'

'The occasion of your marriage is of very great importance to us all.'

Rashad came to an abrupt halt at the head of the stone staircase. 'My...*marriage?*'

'Our people do not wish to be deprived of a state wedding.'

'Who said that I was married, or even getting married?' Rashad managed to ask in as level a voice as he could muster.

'A journalist contacted your sister, Kalila, in London and showed her a photo taken at the airport. Kalila contacted me and e-mailed that picture of Tilda for us all to see. She is very beautiful and a magnificent surprise. I should have sat up and taken more notice the day I heard you were having the old palace refurbished!'

Rashad was thinking fast and realising that so many facts were already out in the family and public arena that he could not simply dismiss the story out of hand. He had been frankly appalled by the presence of the paparazzi at Heathrow—

the rumours must have been flying around about his relationship with Tilda before he'd even got his jet off the ground in London! So much for discretion and privacy! He was even more taken aback by his father's hearty enthusiasm at the news that his son had married a woman he had never met.

'When you proclaimed that Tilda was your woman and required no visa, old Butrus almost had a heart attack until it dawned on him that you must already be married to her to make such an announcement. And, even had you not been—' the king chuckled in the best of good humour '—according to the laws of our royal house once you declared Tilda yours before witnesses, it was a marriage by declaration. The statute that saved your grandfather's skin was never repealed.'

Rashad found it necessary to lean back against the wall for support. A marriage by declaration—a law hastily trotted out to clean up the scandal after his licentious grandfather had run off with his grandmother with not the slightest intention of doing anything other than bedding her. It was still legal? He felt as if the bars of a cage were closing round him.

'My father…' Rashad breathed in deep.

'As if you would bring any woman other than your intended bride into Bakhar!' the older man quipped. 'No man of honour would sully a woman's reputation. I had only to hear Tilda's name spoken and at once I knew she was your bride and that we had a wonderful celebration to arrange. Was she not the woman who gained your heart five years ago?'

As the king waxed lyrical on the subjects of true love and lifelong matrimonial happiness Rashad grew a great deal grimmer at his end of the phone. There might be sunlight beyond the window, but a giant dark cloud was now obscuring his appreciation of it. He had broken the rules only once and now he was to pay the price with his freedom. What insanity had seized him when he had taken the risk of bringing Tilda into Bakhar? It had been an act of utter recklessness and, in retrospect, he could not fathom what had driven him to the point of such incredible folly.

Rashad went downstairs to greet the Prime Minister and his entourage. He accepted hearty congratulations, elaborate greetings and compliments for his bride and the news that a two-day public holiday had already been declared at the end of the month to mark the occasion of his state wedding. He did not even pale when he was informed that formal announcements had been made on the state television and radio services and that bridal good wishes were pouring in from every corner of Bakhar.

It was a full hour before he was in a position to return to Tilda. He was still suffering all the outrage and disbelief of a male who had never put a foot wrong in his life, but now had made one fatal error. He had no doubt whatsoever that Tilda would be ecstatic at the news that she was not a concubine but a wife, and that at the very least they would have to stay married for a year.

Fully dressed, Tilda was pacing the floor. Sporadic outbreaks of gunfire and the extraordinary amount of air traffic had frightened her into wondering if the palace was under attack. When silence had fallen, she had finally succumbed to the most sickening fear that Rashad had not re-appeared because he had been taken prisoner, wounded or killed. Her response to that suspicion was much more emotional than she would have liked to admit and had informed her that her hatred ran only skin deep. While it was perfectly all right to loathe Rashad when he was in front of her and enjoying full health, when she was assailed by a vision of him lying somewhere hurt and unattended she felt sick and wanted to rush to his aid. For that reason, she was on the very brink of disobeying orders and leaving the room when the door opened.

'Where on earth have you been all this time?' she shot at Rashad in instant fury at his reappear-ance, when it became immediately obvious that her fears had been nonsensical: not a strand of his luxuriant black hair was out of place and his superb tailored suit was immaculate. 'I've been frantic with worry!'

'Why?' Rashad asked, ebony brows pleating.

'The gunfire…your instructions…all those jets and helicopters flying in and round about!' Tilda slung at him shakily.

'There is no cause for alarm. Natural caution urged me to ask you to stay here. But the outbreak of excitement was a celebration and the result of a misapprehension.' Rashad shrugged a broad shoulder with something less than his usual cool. 'The misunderstanding is entirely my fault. The whole country thinks that I have brought you back to Bakhar as my wife.'

Tilda was so taken aback by that information that she simply stared at him, noting that his lean, strong face was unusually pale and taut. 'For goodness sake, why would anyone think something like that?'

'Circumstances have conspired to make it the only acceptable interpretation of events,' Rashad pronounced with great care. 'I acknowledge that I did wrong in bringing you here. No woman has ever travelled home to Bakhar with me before. The intervention of the press in London and their awareness of our previous relationship only added strength to the rumour that you are, at the very least, my intended bride.'

Tilda blinked. 'So what now?'

Rashad frowned. 'According to my father we are already married in the eyes of the law, because I referred to you as my woman in front of witnesses.'

Puzzled by the first part of that explanation, Tilda easily picked up on the second part and slung him an angry look of disdain. 'You called me *that*? When?'

'Before we alighted from the jet. But I can put my hand on my heart and swear on my honour that I intended no insult to you.'

'Of course you did—you described me as your woman as though I was a possession! It's medieval!'

'You feel as though you belong with me. I meant that you were part of my life,' Rashad growled. 'Now you are in truth a part.'

'In the eyes of the law…we're *already married?*' Tilda parroted in sudden shock as his original meaning finally sank in on her. 'How can that be?'

'Many years ago, my grandfather abducted my grandmother and created a huge scandal. He always acted first and thought afterwards. To smooth matters over it was considered necessary to pass a law that allowed him to claim that she was his wife from the moment he said she was in the presence of witnesses. That law relates only to the royal family and it has not been repealed.'

'But such behaviour and laws of that sort are still downright medieval! With relations like that, I'm amazed that you had the nerve to criticise *my* family.' Tilda shook her head in a daze, her thoughts tumbling about in turmoil while she attempted to reason with clarity. 'Well, the obvious solution to all this ridiculous confusion is that you just tell the truth. You are, after all, *very* fond of telling me that lies are always unacceptable to you.'

As that proposal was made, a tiny muscle pulled taut at the corner of Rashad's unsmiling mouth. 'The truth would now appear to be that, according to Bakhari law, we are legally married.'

'If that is so, I really do think that it would serve you right,' Tilda admitted helplessly. 'But, as I wouldn't stay married to you even if you had a gun to my head, the divorce can't come quick enough!'

'This is a serious matter.'

A bitter edge had already entered Tilda's thoughts and coloured them. She was remembering how madly in love she had been five years earlier. In those days she would've made any sacrifice to marry her desert prince. Were they really and truly married? No doubt that fact explained why he was as grave as though he were attending a funeral. She was obviously the very last woman alive that he would have willingly chosen to be his wife.

'I expect it is serious. But if I'm married to you, then I must have some rights.' Her beautiful eyes concealed by her lashes, she turned her head away from him, determined not to reveal that she was upset. 'Or have you got another list of threats to hold over me to ensure that I do exactly as you want me to do?'

That candid question hit Rashad like a bucket of icy water on hot skin. Until she had come back into his life, he had never threatened a woman, nor ever dreamt that he might do so. Now he was confronted head-on with his harsh treatment of Tilda. Once, she had betrayed his trust and inflicted a wound for which he had never forgiven her. But that, Rashad acknowledged heavily, was no defence for a misuse of power to mete out punishment. His father's talk of marriage and the photo of Tilda with Jerrold had reawakened Rashad's bitter anger and encouraged him to pursue what he believed to be justice. But from the instant he had seen Tilda again, far less acceptable motives and desires had powered him. No longer could he marvel at the disastrous consequences that he had unleashed on both of them.

'No. There will be no more threats.' His lean and darkly handsome face sober, Rashad surveyed her with dark, unreadable eyes. 'I should never have used coercive tactics.'

Surprised by that total turnaround, Tilda lifted her pale blond head. 'You're admitting that?'

'I can do nothing less when I look at the situation I have created. I was in the wrong and for that I apologise.' Voicing those words of sincere regret cost Rashad a great deal of pride for he had never had to apologise before. 'I harboured anger from the past and it blinded me to what was right.'

Tilda could only think of her own anger, nourished and kept alive by hurt. She thought of the fact that she had never let any man so close to her again. She thought of how she had felt just minutes earlier when she had been afraid that he might have been injured. A giant tide of fear engulfed her at that point as she appreciated that her feelings for Rashad ran much deeper than was safe or sensible.

'I will never threaten you again,' Rashad promised her levelly. 'Instead, I am asking you for your co-operation.'

'Are we really and truly married?' Tilda prompted uncertainly.

'Yes,' Rashad confirmed.

'But I expect you'll do whatever it takes to get us out of the marriage as fast as you possibly can,' Tilda remarked in a tone that was a tad brittle.

Rashad studied the wall to one side of her with frowning attention. Divorce would entail her departure from Bakhar. He discovered that that prospect had no appeal for him whatsoever. Surely, he reasoned, a hasty marriage and an even hastier divorce would only compound the errors he had made? A marriage was a marriage, no matter how it had been entered into. In the same way a wife was a wife, deserving of his support and respect. He should at least try to make a success of their alliance, he decided with sudden purpose. He would have to learn to put all memory of her past behind him.

'A quick divorce is not an option I would wish to choose.' Rashad rested dark golden eyes, gleaming with renewed energy, back on her. 'There is no reason why we should not attempt to make the best of our predicament.'

'Meaning?' Suddenly maddeningly aware of the smouldering appraisal resting on the swollen contours of her pink mouth, Tilda tensed. Without warning she found that she was reliving the melting pleasure of his hungry mouth roaming over her breasts and the pulsing ache at the secret heart of her body. She sucked in a fractured breath, embarrassed by her susceptibility.

Taut with arousal, Rashad made a valiant attempt to overcome the barrier of his fierce pride and build a bridge that might take him from coercion to acceptance. He moved closer. 'Waking or sleeping, you are in my every thought. My hunger for you is no greater than yours for me. I want to be with you.'

Tilda swallowed the lump in her throat and hated herself for being tempted. But he was only interested in getting her into bed. That was all he had ever been interested in, she told herself wretchedly. Yet her body still tingled with the sexual responsiveness that only he could awaken. It incensed her that she knew exactly what he was talking about. Every day, every hour, her every thought was centred on him, to the point of obsession. But that was a truth she despised and would never admit to him.

In any case, she had much more important things to worry about. Within the space of an hour every seeming certainty had vanished. It seemed shameful to her that she should long to walk into his arms and forget everything both past and present because of passion. What would sharing a bed with Rashad fix or clarify? Where were her pride and her common sense? First and foremost, she was in Bakhar for the sake of her family. She reminded herself that she had yet to see evidence that the threat against their security had been lifted.

'What I need right now is the assurance that that eviction order has been cancelled,' she murmured tautly.

A faint rise of dark blood marking the angular line of his classic cheekbones, Rashad fell still. 'It has been.'

As the tense pool of silence gathered Tilda worried uncomfortably at her full lower lip. 'And the house—has it been signed back to my mother?'

'Of course.'

'The outstanding loan has been settled?'

Rashad inclined his proud dark head in immediate acknowledgement.

'I would like to see all that in writing.' Tilda closed her restive hands together in front of her. In an effort to conceal her discomfiture, she was struggling to be as businesslike as he had once urged her to be.

'If that is your wish. I will ensure that you see the documentation.' Affronted though he was by that lack of trust in his word, Rashad made no further comment. He told himself that he should not be surprised that financial matters were her first consideration. Had he not always known that money meant more to her than anything else? He could not quell the rise of his distaste.

Tilda's fingers curled in on themselves too tightly for comfort. 'And I would also like to see the proof you said you had of my affairs with other men.'

Rashad veiled his icy gaze, determined not to surrender to that particular demand. Confronting

her with unassailable evidence of her youthful promiscuity would only antagonise her at a time when
he needed her co-operation. If she refused to
conduct herself as his wife, his father and the rest
of his family would be, at the very least, severely
embarrassed. Indeed, all too many innocent people
were at risk of suffering the consequences of his
bad judgement and lack of foresight.

'I'm afraid that's not possible.'

He looked apologetic and he sounded apologetic, but Tilda was not convinced. She was parting
her lips to tell him so when he voiced an apology
at the interruption and answered his mobile phone.

His lean bronzed profile taut, he compressed
his wide, sensual mouth. 'My sisters, Durra and
Tibah, have arrived.'

In a large reception room downstairs she was
immediately approached by two fashionably
dressed women, who looked to be in their forties
and, as such, a good deal older than Tilda had
expected. Both spoke excellent English and
greeted their brother with an affection laced with
deferential restraint.

'The king has asked that you bring Tilda to him today so that he can meet her.' A small plump brunette with a bustling air, Durra greeted Tilda with warm words of welcome.

'There are a great many preparations to be made,' Tibah added with enthusiasm. 'The next few weeks will be very exciting! I do hope you can come now. We try not to keep our father waiting.'

Tilda noticed that Rashad looked very much as though he had been carved out of solid granite. Her heart and self-image slowly sank to her toes while she kept a resolute smile pinned to her taut mouth. She was painfully aware of Rashad's low opinion of her and felt that he could only loathe the prospect of introducing her as his bride to the father he esteemed. His siblings regarded him with barely concealed tension until he inclined his sleek dark head in agreement. He clapped his hands and a servant appeared from beyond the door. He issued instructions.

'We will leave immediately,' he murmured without expression.

His sisters flew back to Jumiah with them. The Great Palace where the royal family lived was situated several miles outside the flourishing capital city. As soon as the helicopter landed, Durra and Tibah parted from Rashad and Tilda to return to their apartments within the palace complex. A vast carved stone building enhanced by formal gardens and fountains, it was a much newer property than Tilda had expected to see and she made a surprised comment.

'The old palace was badly damaged during the war. It had also taken on unfortunate associations after two decades of my great-uncle's misrule,' Rashad explained. 'This new palace was built as a symbol of hope for the future.'

'It's colossal but very impressive.' Tilda shot him a strained glance and suddenly abandoned the stilted conversation in favour of honesty. 'Is there no way I can avoid having to meet your father?'

His stubborn jaw line clenched hard. 'In wishing to admit you so immediately to his presence, the king seeks to honour you.'

Tilda went pink with discomfiture. 'You mis-understood my meaning. Oh, never mind.'

'My father is a kind man. Not unreasonably, he has assumed that there is honest affection between us.'

The backs of Tilda's eyes stung in receipt of that sardonic reminder but she lifted her chin. To add insult to injury, Rashad proceeded to give her several tips on how to be polite and respectful in the presence of Bakhari royalty. 'There's nothing wrong with my manners,' she told him tightly. 'I'm not going to be rude.'

'I did not intend to cause offence.' Rashad was merely annoyed that she should have to enter such a crucial meeting without any preparation whatsoever.

Feeling wretchedly unsuitable for the honour being extended to her, Tilda was ushered into the audience room. King Hazar was a tall, spare man in his sixties, garbed in traditional robes that added to his quiet aura of dignity. The kind-liness of his unexpectedly friendly smile took her aback and instantly released the worst of her tension. He welcomed her to Bakhar in slow, careful English, embraced his son with enthusiasm and informed Tilda that he would be happy to regard her as another daughter. Very polite conversation ensued about the sights of Oxford, as well as the vagaries of the English climate. It dawned on Tilda that, far from being aghast at or even worried by his son's sudden marriage to an Englishwoman, the older man seemed genuinely delighted.

Under cover of this gentle dialogue, she studied Rashad from below her lashes. His lean bronzed profile was lit by the sunshine piercing the window behind him. As if aware of her attention, he turned his arrogant dark head. His tawny gaze met hers and her tummy performed an instant somersault of response. Colouring, she dragged her attention from him again. Goodness, he was gorgeous, she thought helplessly, and she was married to him. Really and truly married. The shock of that was still sinking in. With difficulty she returned her concentration to the conversation.

Rashad was wondering to himself exactly why his royal parent was so overjoyed by his supposed marriage. Had the older man feared that his son would remain single for the rest of his days? Was almost any wife better than no wife on his father's terms? Was that why not a single awkward question had yet been asked of either of them?

The king said that it was of great importance that Tilda receive support and guidance to enable her to feel at home within the royal household and in the country beyond the palace walls. 'Unlike your late mother, your wife will lead a life in the public eye,' his father remarked gravely. 'It is only sensible that Tilda should be helped to prepare for that role in advance of your wedding.'

What wedding? Tilda almost asked, just managing to bite back the startled query, for she was very much afraid of saying the wrong thing. She stole another covert glance at Rashad and noted that he seemed quite unfazed by that same reference. She suspected that he might be rationing information on a strict need-to-know basis and resentment stirred in her.

'I'm not convinced that Tilda should take on a public role,' Rashad countered.

Tilda tried to ignore Rashad's lack of enthusiasm for her taking on the responsibilities that went with being his wife. Naturally he felt like that, she told herself impatiently. There was no need whatsoever for her to take that personally. Unhappily this common-sense conviction did not prevent her from feeling cut to the bone and deemed a loser before she even got to run the race.

His father looked amused. 'My son, you cannot marry an educated and accomplished young lady and hope to keep her all to yourself. Why, the crown office has already had a request for your wife to open the new surgical wing of the hospital next month! All such matters will be more easily dealt with if Tilda has had the opportunity to study our history, etiquette and language, so that she may be comfortable wherever she travels within our borders.'

In the aftermath of the revealing meeting, Tilda was in a tense and unhappy daze. It appeared that some big fancy wedding was in the offing to satisfy convention. The very idea of that made her feel uncomfortable, because she was no actress. What was more, pretending to be Rashad's wife promised to be a serious challenge. Evidently it was regarded as something of a full-time occupation if she was to be put in training for the role. But, worst of all, Rashad was expecting her to take part in a massive pretence and enact a cruelly deceptive masquerade to fool people who were trustingly offering her sincere affection and acceptance. His family all seemed so *nice!* In her opinion only a truly horrid and insensitive person could feel anything other than guilt-stricken.

CHAPTER SEVEN

'YOU did very well with my father. He was most impressed,' Rashad commented, resting a lean hand at the base of Tilda's spine to guide her in the direction of his wing of the palace.

'I was so nervous I hardly said a word,' Tilda confided anxiously. 'I know next to nothing about you and your family and I was terrified of saying something that would reveal that. Your sisters are older than I expected. Why did you never talk about your family when you were a student?'

'Five years ago, my father and my sisters still felt like strangers to me.'

'But why?' Tilda questioned in bewilderment.

'My three sisters are the children of my father's first wife, who died of a fever after

Kalila's birth. I am the son of his second marriage. When I was four years old my father was badly hurt in a riding accident,' Rashad explained. 'His uncle Sadiq stepped in as Regent and then used the opportunity to take the throne by force. My father was still bedridden when Sadiq took me from my family and held me as a hostage.'

'For how long?'

'Until I was an adult. Sadiq had no son of his own and he named me as his heir to keep certain factions happy. I was sent to a military academy and then I went into the army. My family's safety was dependent on Sadiq's goodwill.'

Tilda was appalled. 'My goodness, why did you never tell me any of this before? I mean, I knew about Sadiq and the war, but I didn't realise you'd been separated from your family when you were only a little boy.'

'I have never seen the wisdom of dwelling on misfortunes.'

'Your mother must have been devastated.'

'I believe so. I never saw her again. She fell ill

when I was a teenager but I was not allowed to visit her.'

For perhaps the first time, Tilda understood the source of the unrelenting strength and self-discipline that lay at the heart of Rashad's character. As a child he must have suffered great loneliness and grief at being denied his family and it had hardened him. He had learnt to hide his emotions and make an idol of self-sufficiency. It was little wonder that he did not give his trust easily.

They crossed a marble forecourt screened by trees and lush vegetation. Daylight was fading as the sun slowly sank in a spectacularly beautiful sky shot with shades of peach, tangerine and ochre. Beyond the extensive greenery sat a substantial building. 'My home here at the palace is extremely private,' Rashad remarked.

In a magnificent circular entrance hall large enough to stage a concert, Tilda came to a halt. 'The king mentioned something about a wedding.'

Rashad waved away the eager and curious

servants who had all clustered below the stairs, and whom Tilda did not notice. He pushed open a door and stepped back. Tilda preceded him into a very large reception room decorated very much in the Eastern style with sumptuous sofas and a carpet so exquisite that it seemed a sin to actually walk on it.

'There will be a state wedding held for us at the end of the month. It cannot be avoided,' Rashad murmured. 'My people expect such a show and to do otherwise would be to create a great deal of comment.'

Tilda was rigid with disbelief, but she made no immediate response. She felt as though she were sinking into quicksand and only she was aware of the emergency. She could not credit that he simply expected her to go along with all such arrangements as though they were a genuine couple!

Rashad continued to pursue his deliberate policy of politely ignoring the tense signals Tilda was emanating. If he set an example, it was possible that in time she would learn to mirror his behaviour. 'May I call for dinner to be served?' he asked. 'I don't know about you, but it seems like a very long time since we last ate a proper meal and I confess that I am hungry.'

That reference to food was the proverbial last straw for Tilda. Her tension gave suddenly as she spread her hands wide in a helpless gesture of frustration. 'I can't do this, Rashad…I really can't! How do you manage to act as though everything's normal?'

'Discipline,' he told her quietly.

'Well, it's freaky and unnatural,' Tilda told him feelingly. 'We have to talk about this—'

'Why? Nothing can be changed. We're married. I am your husband. You are my wife. We must do what is expected of us.'

'Sacrifice doesn't come naturally to those of us who were not raised to be royal and perfect!' Tilda declared.

His strong jaw line set. 'I am not trying to be perfect.'

'Your father and your sisters are lovely. What a welcome they've given me!' Tilda shook her silvery fair head, struggling to find the right words with which to voice her deep unease at the role that had been forced on her. 'Doesn't deceiving them into believing that we're a real couple bother you?'

'Of course it does, but it is the lesser of two evils. I can only regret the actions that brought us to this point. But I also accept that the truth would shame and distress, not only my family, but also our people. A respectful pretence is the best option on offer to us.'

Tilda was very tempted to look for something large and heavy and throw it at him in the hope of extracting a less logical and dispassionate response. 'But this is a total nightmare.'

Accustomed to her love of exaggeration, Rashad surveyed her with glinting golden eyes of appreciation. Even after a day that would have taxed most women to the edge of hysteria she still looked absolutely amazing: glorious hair, glorious skin, glorious eyes, glowing and full of life. Out of politeness, courtiers, government officials and staff had tried not to stare at her, but the pure impact of her beauty had proved too much for many. That she had not betrayed the smallest awareness of that attention had impressed him. He had felt proud of her.

'Not a nightmare,' Rashad chided gently.

'Well, it is a nightmare for me!' Tilda condemned, her temper finally letting rip in the face of such indifference to her feelings. 'I don't routinely lie to people. I can't feel comfortable faking stuff. I don't have the first idea about how to act like your wife—'

'I can help you. You should have entered our apartments, met the servants and accepted their flowers and congratulations. You would then have ordered dinner.'

Her generous pink mouth fell wide. What servants? She had not seen any servants! And why was he talking about food again? After a day when she had reeled dizzily from one shock into the next, was that truly all he could think about?

'Or, you could have gone straight upstairs with me to bed,' Rashad framed, willing to exchange one hunger for another that became more pressing every time he looked at her. His intent gaze acquired a smouldering light as it roamed over her lovely face and slim, shapely figure. 'I can tell you now that sex is a high priority on my list. Meet my expectations there and I will regard you as the perfect wife.'

Tilda was almost dumbfounded with rage. For once, she could see that he had had no thought of being facetious. He was set on being candid and helpful when he informed her that his priorities were as basic as Neanderthal man's had no doubt been. Sex and food.

'I do not aspire to be the perfect wife, and if that was the pep talk that was supposed to act as inspiration it was a killer!' Tilda launched at him. 'You asked for my co-operation. As I seemed to have very little choice, I went along with that, but I had no idea how big a charade you were expecting me to dish up!'

Lean, darkly handsome face taut, Rashad breathed, 'Our marriage does not have to be a charade.'

'And I don't have to be a concubine within this stupid fake marriage if I don't want to be!'

Tilda flung that declaration and folded her arms, pride and fortitude prompting her to take a stand. She was willing to co-operate when it came to the marriage ceremony, but that was enough. Anything more than co-operation would have to be earned. Rashad was at the very foot of that particular learning curve…and his hints about sex and food were unlikely to increase his chances of achievement.

'Tilda…'

'Just you dare say one more word about how best to meet your expectations and, I swear, I'll scream until you gag me!' Tilda threatened, her voice half an octave higher in tone. 'You're not persuading me. You are so spoilt, so used to women who fall over themselves to do whatever you want—'

'Where am I going wrong with you? Perhaps I'm talking too much when action would be preferable.' Strolling forward, Rashad treated her to a fierce look of masculine challenge and, without hesitation, he pulled her into his arms.

Tilda was so disconcerted by that move in the middle of their argument that she lost valuable seconds when she might have gone into retreat. In the interim, Rashad ravished her mouth with his and set off a shattering sexual chain reaction throughout her slender body. Even though she knew she should not, she kissed him back, bruising her lips with the wild hot urgency that had risen like a crazy fever inside her, her hands delving into his black hair like possessive claws. She wanted him, wanted him, *wanted* him…just like a concubine? A favourite concubine? Those mocking words and the memory of how he had threatened to teach her to beg for his sexual attention, returned to haunt her. In an abrupt movement she tore herself free of his lithe hard body and literally tottered away a few steps on legs that didn't feel strong enough to keep her upright.

Rashad was trembling, his body screaming for release. *You're not persuading me,* she had said. Outrage roared through him when he grasped the significance of those words. What was it that Tilda found persuasive? What did it take to make Tilda surrender? As the answer came his fists clenched and he hated her as much as he wanted her and the force of that internal turmoil threatened to rip him apart.

'How much?' he intoned in a wrathful undertone. 'How much of a financial inducement do you want to share my bed?'

Shock at that question turned Tilda's flushed face white. Did he still think so little of her? Of course he did. Had she not agreed to sleep with him in return for having a very large debt written off? Her fire of anger was doused, but she was appalled at being directly confronted with his belief that she would do anything for cash.

'I don't want your money,' she whispered tightly, forcing out the denial between tremulous lips. 'Please don't make me an offer like that ever again.'

Rashad was eager to believe that he had misinterpreted her behaviour. 'Then why do you deny us what we both desire?'

Sucking in a steadying breath, Tilda spun back to him, her bright eyes veiled to a wary glimmer. 'Sex isn't so simple for me as it is for you. I may have been willing to protect my family at the cost of my pride, but I'm not for sale any more. I'm sorry if you think that's dishonest,' she muttered defensively, 'but I think that it's a fair enough exchange if I agree to act like your wife and jump through all the right hoops to please everyone. I'll keep up the performance for as long as you ask, as well. That will be enough of a challenge when I can't possibly think of myself as your wife in any real way.'

Striving to control his hunger for her, Rashad regarded her with passionate force. 'Did I misunderstand what you meant by persuasion?'

A strangulated laugh was wrenched from Tilda. 'Oh, yes. But don't worry about it. All I'm asking for is a separate bedroom.'

'And that is what you want?' Rashad was frowning. He could barely credit what she was saying. She was his wife. She already *felt* like his wife. Was that really how she felt?

'*All* that I want from you, believe me.' Tilda would not look at him again for she had little faith in what she was saying even though pride had demanded that she say it. She wanted him with every fibre of her being but she would not let herself sink to the level of sleeping with a man who assumed he might have to pay her for his pleasure. He was his own worst enemy, she thought painfully. A few pleasing words, even a fleeting reference to the beauty of the desert sunset, and he could have had her for nothing. But flattery and romantic allusions to sunsets had never been Rashad's style.

'It will be as you wish. I have work to do. Excuse me,' Rashad responded with scrupulous politeness.

The door closed and the silence folded in. She expelled her breath in a long jagged surge. Her fingers lifted to the reddened and tingling contours of her lips and something like a sob tugged at her vocal cords, forcing her to grit her teeth and fight for self-control.

She dined solitarily later that evening in a state dining room with superb marble walls and floor. She ate everything that was put in front of her and tasted nothing. What had gone so badly wrong between herself and Rashad that he could think she was so cheap? Why was he so convinced that she had gone with other men behind his back? He was logical, intelligent. What was the proof of her infidelity that he evidently considered irrefutable? She knew that for the sake of her self-esteem she had to find out.

Sitting there alone, she remembered how madly in love with Rashad she had once been. She recalled cherished memories of fun, sweetness and passion. Once, a car had backfired in the street. Assuming that it was gunfire, Rashad had thrown her to the ground and protected her with his body. The sheepish expression on his face in the aftermath had been comic, but she had been touched to the heart to realise that, at a moment when he had honestly believed that he was in danger, he had instinctively put her safety before his own.

Nobody had ever really tried to look after Tilda before and, although she had scoffed at the idea, she had liked it because, for too long, she'd had to be the strong one in her family and look out for everyone else's interests. She had leant on Rashad and found him wonderfully supportive, even while the power of her passion for him had terrified her as much as it excited her. Determined not to be hurt, she had believed that she was in full control of her emotions. Then, out of the blue, he had dumped her and all her proud illusions had crumbled faster than the speed of light.

One day everything had seemed fine, the next it had been over. Rashad had arranged to take out her for a meal. She had sat waiting for him to pick her up. Time had crept on and he hadn't arrived, hadn't phoned, either. She had tried to call him on his mobile and there had been no answer. The next day, frantic with worry that something had happened to him, she had called round at the house he had rented and his staff had refused her entry. No explanation, no apology, nothing. Believing that in some way she must have offended him, she had gotten angry then and had decided to sit him out. For several days she had lived in denial of her growing misery until, one evening, when she just hadn't been able to bear being without him any longer, she had found out from a friend where he was and had gone in search of him.

The party had been at Leonidas Pallis's apartment. Through the crush, she had seen Rashad on a sofa with a sinuous redhead wrapped round him. Rashad, who supposedly didn't like such public displays of intimacy, had been kissing the girl. Something had died inside Tilda and all her proud pretences had fallen apart as she had fought her passage back to the exit. She had been convinced that he had ditched her and replaced her with a more sexually available girlfriend. There had been a desperate irony to the fact that it had been only then that she had fully appreciated how much she loved him.

As Tilda let herself recall the terrible hurt of Rashad's betrayal five years earlier, her chin came up. No way was she going to give Rashad the chance to put her through those agonies again! She might still be drawn to him like a stupid moth to a candle flame, but that didn't mean she had to surrender to her weakness or let him suspect that it existed. Events had made them more equal, she told herself bracingly. She was trading co-operation rather than sex in return for the debts he had written off. At least being partners in a pretend marriage left her with some dignity and he was already discovering that he could not treat a wife like a concubine.

Tilda straightened her slight shoulders, turquoise eyes luminous with purpose. She might not feel as though they were married but, goodness, she intended to be the *perfect* wife in public. By the time she left Bakhar, Prince Rashad Hussein Al-Zafar and his family would feel that he was losing a woman who had been an absolute solid gold asset to him. And not if he offered her a million pounds, not even if he begged on his knees, would she stay with him!

CHAPTER EIGHT

IN THE privacy of his office, Rashad watched the film footage for the third time. The camera, obviously wielded by a man hopelessly enthralled with Tilda's exquisite face, followed her every move at a children's concert. In front of a camera she was a natural and highly photogenic, and the Bakhari media industry had succumbed to their first bout of celebrity fever. When his sisters had taken Tilda shopping in Jumiah, the traffic had been brought to a standstill because interest in Tilda had been so great that drivers had abandoned their cars to try and catch a glimpse of her in the flesh.

Alarmed by the size of the crowds that had swiftly formed that morning, Rashad had wasted no time in tripling the size of Tilda's protection team. He had also put a more experienced man in charge of her security. She was incredibly popular. He ran the footage of the concert again and absorbed the lingering shots of his wife's radiant smile, her relaxed warmth with the children and the interest she showed in everyone she spoke to. Her intelligence and charisma attracted much admiring comment. Tilda might now look like a beautiful fashion queen, but when a toddler left a sandy handprint on her dress she just laughed and brushed herself down. In less than a month she had become the best-known face in Bakhar, next to his father's and his own.

So, who was it who had said that the camera never lied? Was this the same woman who had once deceived him, extracted money from him and slept with other men? Was the fact that she *still* hadn't slept with him ongoing evidence of the existence of that other unscrupulous persona? Was she simply a fantastic actress? Was she giving the people what they wanted, just as she had once played the innocent for his benefit? After all, he was willing to concede her innocence was what he had wanted most when he'd first met her. Then, he had been too idealistic to desire a succession of different women in his bed. What he had wanted most was a wife. Tilda had struck him as a pearl beyond price and he had put her on a pedestal.

Lean, powerful face grim, Rashad froze Tilda's image on screen. The woman in the film was a more adult version of the girl he remembered and he was deeply disturbed by the fact. Second time round, armed with the knowledge of her greed and promiscuity, he had expected to easily detect her insincerity and her other flaws. But Tilda was contriving to keep her dark side remarkably well hidden from him and from the whole of Bakhar. Few people were all bad or all good, he reminded himself impatiently. Wasn't it possible that she had seen the error of her ways and changed them? How could he doubt her guilt even for a moment? For wasn't that what was really bothering him? He had so far failed to match the woman enchanting everyone with her charm with the greedy, scheming wanton she was supposed to be at heart.

In a sudden movement Rashad straightened to his full height and unlocked the safe. He had to go right to the back of it to find the slim security file he sought. Put together by a British private detective, it was written in English. Rashad remembered what a battle he had had to understand that language on the day he'd read it and shock had made his brain freeze. He still felt queasy just looking at the cover of the file with her name on it. He reminded himself that it had come to him direct from an impeccable source. He felt that he needed to read it again, but he believed it would be unduly disrespectful to Tilda to even open that unsavoury file now, two days before their wedding.

His tension eased, his brilliant gaze simmered gold. The day after tomorrow, Tilda would be one hundred per cent his. She would have no grounds to complain of medieval laws and customs. There could be no suggestion that their union was anything other than legal and above-board. A wolfish smile of satisfaction slashed his wide, sensual mouth. Aware that he needed her co-operation before their state wedding made them the most married couple in Bakhar, he had played a waiting game of restraint. But restraint had its limits: his bride would lie in his bed on their wedding night.

The phone rang to inform him that Tilda's family were about to arrive. Rashad glanced at the file still in his hand and thrust it into his briefcase. Determined to award her mother and siblings every courtesy and frankly curious to meet them all again, Rashad left his office to be at Tilda's side. He had not actually been invited to be so, but he was prepared to rise above that small slight.

Tilda wrapped her arms exuberantly round Katie and Megan and had she had a third arm she would have hugged her brother James, as well, who gave her hair an affectionate tug and stepped back out of reach with a laughing complaint when she tried to hug him. Aubrey was shaking his head over the astonishing splendour and size of the palace.

'So much for the accounting job you mentioned!' Katie teased. 'Here you are decked out
in designer gear, living in the lap of luxury and
about to marry the love of your life. Obviously
you took one look at each other and went over-
board again. The only thing that stops it all being
perfect is Mum not being here with us.'

Tilda sighed in agreement. 'I know. She's
ecstatic that I'm getting married to Rashad but
really sad she can't be here with us.'

'Mum is a lot happier and less nervy,' the
youthful blonde confided. 'Aubrey thinks that
having to miss your wedding might be just what
it takes to push her into getting the professional
help she needs.'

Having chatted to her parent regularly on the
phone since leaving home, Tilda was well aware
that Beth was in a much healthier and stronger
frame of mind since she had been able to stop
worrying about her debts. Stress, Tilda thought
ruefully, might well have made her mother's
condition worse. An end to Scott's threatening
visits would also have helped.

'Rashad!' Megan suddenly yelled and tore across the room, only to fall still in sudden uncertainty several feet from the male she had once idolised.

Laughing at that noisy and enthusiastic welcome, Rashad strode straight up to the girl and bent down to speak to her.

'He's, like, totally the fairy-tale prince.' Katie rolled admiring eyes and groaned. 'So handsome, likes kids, always polite and charming. I mean, why the heck did you two ever break up? A silly row?'

'Something like that.'

'There's something that you should know. Remember the reporters cornering you at the airport?' Katie murmured uneasily. 'That was James's fault and he feels awful about it.'

'How on earth could it have been James's fault?' Tilda questioned.

'Dad—Scott.' Katie grimaced. 'James phones Scott sometimes, and James let drop about you and Rashad. It's a fair bet that Scott passed on the news to someone, maybe made a bit of money out of it.'

Tilda was relieved to find out who had been responsible, but disturbed by the fact that her younger brother had been in contact with his father. She took a deep breath and told her sister that Scott had been taking money from their mother. Katie scolded Tilda for not telling her sooner and promised to warn James.

Tilda found her attention roaming back continually to Rashad. His arrival had bowled her over. It was a challenge to take her eyes off his lean, darkly beautiful features. But then, she had seen precious little of him over the past month. Her days had been filled with history, language and etiquette lessons, not to mention dress fittings, shopping trips, innumerable social meetings with Rashad's extended family and several informal public appearances.

Every night she had fallen into bed exhausted and lain awake listening in vain for Rashad coming home, because his bedroom was so far from hers that she had no hope of hearing his return. Slowly but surely, his cool detachment had begun to infuriate her. A member of his staff had brought her a sealed envelope containing all the documents pertaining to the transfer of the family home back into her mother's name and the writing off of the loan. She had sent him a very polite note of thanks.

But it had not achieved the desired response, for he had not come looking for her. She had more or less told him to leave her alone and Rashad, who had never, ever done what she told him to do before, *was* leaving her alone. Initially she had told herself that this proved that there had been no real substance to his assurance that their marriage did not have to be a charade. But it had soon dawned on her that demanding a separate bedroom had been a sure-fire way of ensuring that their relationship remained a sham. Though it galled her to admit it, she wanted much more from him.

Rashad's working day began very early. A lie-in had become an unknown treat for Tilda because the minute Rashad left the building she raced down the corridor and across a court-yard to his room to check that his bed had actually been occupied the night before. Well aware that he had a very racy reputation as a womaniser, Tilda had developed a need to continually check that he wasn't doing anything suspicious. She was now as well acquainted with Rashad's daily schedule as any seasoned member of his staff.

He rose at five in the morning to go riding across the desert sands. He showered at six. He often breakfasted and dined with his father, or had a working meal with staff. He rarely ate lunch. He worked extremely hard. He had gone abroad on business twice and she hadn't slept a wink while he was away for worrying that he might be making up for those weeks of celibacy. Every day he sent her flowers or, if he had seen little of her, he phoned her. If she was silent or sulky, he did the talking. His manners were outrageously good, his reserve impenetrable. She was convinced that he could hold a pleasant conversation with a brick wall. He remained breathtakingly impervious to her most tart remarks. At times, she had wanted to screech down the phone like a shrew to get a reaction from him but if that had happened she'd have felt horribly childish.

Now she watched him speaking to each of her siblings and receiving an overwhelmingly positive response from each of them. He was good with people, quick to set them at their ease, she acknowledged grudgingly. Even Aubrey was smiling and James, often silenced by teenaged awkwardness, was talking away happily.

'Where is your mother?' Rashad asked Tilda in a quiet aside a few minutes later. 'Did the journey overtire her? Has she gone upstairs to lie down?'

Tilda went instantly into defensive mode. 'She's not here. She couldn't come.'

Rashad shot her a perturbed glance. 'Why not?'

Her turquoise eyes sparked. 'I'm not going to tell you and risk being accused of telling sob stories.'

'Tilda,' Rashad chided, gleaming dark as midnight eyes resting on her in level enquiry.

Her face went pink, her mouth running dry. When he looked directly at her a thousand butterflies were set loose in her tummy and it seriously embarrassed her. 'OK. Mum suffers from agoraphobia. It's more than four years since she even went out of the front door of her home. She never goes out. She *can't*.'

His ebony brows pleated in consternation. 'Agoraphobia? You should have told me about this.'

'Why? You were in the process of having my mother evicted. You didn't want the human-interest tales then. It's too late to talk like Mr Compassionate now,' Tilda told him accusingly.

'I was hard on you, but I would never be unjust,' Rashad countered evenly. 'Someone should have given me the true facts of the matter.'

Tilda was determined not to let him off the hook. 'You wouldn't have been interested.'

'I had good reason for mistrust. Five years of inaction followed by a last-minute plea from you? But you must draw a line under that period because your family is now my family. I will do whatever is within my power to ensure that your mother receives the very best treatment available.' Rashad gazed down at Tilda's mutinous

206 THE DESERT SHEIKH'S CAPTIVE WIFE

oval face. 'The day after tomorrow is our wedding day.'

Tilda released a theatrical long-suffering sigh. 'Like I could forget that!'

Rashad flung back his imperious dark head and laughed with genuine appreciation. The day could not come soon enough for him.

'All I can say is…you look amazing,' Katie said dreamily.

Tilda did a little twirl in front of the cheval-mirror. Her wedding gown was glorious: pristine white and cut to enhance her graceful figure, it had the deceptively simple designer elegance that came from style and sumptuous fabric. Her two sisters looked delightful in matching dresses the colour of burnished copper, which had been fitted in London. Rashad's eldest sister, Durra, was acting as a matron of honour for the first ceremony which would be followed by the Bakhari ceremony, a few hours later.

The phone was brought to Tilda. It was her mother, Beth. The older woman's happiness was patent in spite of the thousands of miles that separated mother and daughter. Beth explained that Rashad had arranged for a video link to be set up in her home so that Beth could watch the ceremonies. A lump formed in Tilda's throat. His consideration where her family was concerned was surprising her yet again. Once he had realised that her siblings would be leaving directly after the wedding ceremony because both Aubrey and Katie had exams coming up, he had organised a fun sightseeing tour for them to enjoy the day before.

She rang Rashad to thank him for the video link.

'It was nothing,' he protested.

'It means everything to Mum.' Tilda went into the *en suite* bathroom for privacy and added, 'She thinks this wedding is real, so it's a really big deal for her.'

'For me, as well, and for Bakhar,' Rashad murmured coolly.

'I didn't mean it that way…oh, for goodness' sake, just because you never say *anything* without thinking!' Tilda groaned.

'Tilda?' Katie knocked on the door. 'What are you doing?'

Tilda emerged with sparkling eyes, still talking on the phone. 'Oh, I'm just arguing with Rashad, Katie. Nothing new there—'

'Tilda,' Rashad drawled huskily. 'Make no mistake. This is a real wedding…'

Rashad, devastatingly handsome in a superb grey morning suit, worn with a silk waistcoat and striped trousers, awaited her in a beautifully decorated room filled with all his closest relatives. The Christian marriage service, conducted by a chaplain attached to the British embassy, was short and sweet, but the simple words of the ceremony had a familiarity that had a lingering resonance for Tilda. Rashad slid a platinum ring on her finger and she returned the favour with a matching band on his. For the first time she felt married, for the first time he felt like her husband and she felt like a wife.

'You look fantastic in white,' Rashad confided huskily.

Meeting his appreciative gaze, Tilda tingled. After the bride and groom had posed for formal photographs with King Hazar, Tilda was whisked off at speed to be prepared and pre-sented afresh as a traditional Bakhari bride.

Assisted from her gown by half a dozen pairs of helpful hands, lost in a crowd of chattering women, Tilda was ushered into a palatial bathroom. A scented bath liberally sprinkled with rose petals awaited her. While she bathed, she heard music striking up in the room next door and smiled. There was a marvellous atmosphere of fun in the air. She emerged wrapped in a towel and learnt that she had only completed the first step of the all-important bridal preparations. She submitted to having her hair rinsed with what one of her sisters-in-law ex-plained was an extract of amber and jasmine. It left her tresses silky smooth and deliciously perfumed.

After being placed on a couch, Tilda was gently massaged with aromatic oil and she relaxed for the first time that day. Durra asked her if she would mind having her hands and feet ornamented with henna. Acquiescing, Tilda looked on in fascination while, for the sake of speed, two women embarked on painting delicate lacelike ochre patterns on her slender hands and feet. Refreshing mint tea was served.

'Men are not usually very good at waiting for what they want,' Durra contended cheerfully, 'but Rashad is an exceptional man. It is years since my brother first mentioned your name to us and here you are, his bride at last.'

Surprise made Tilda tense. 'You knew about me then...I mean, Rashad told you about me?'

Durra gave her an anxious apologetic look. 'Perhaps I shouldn't have mentioned it.'

'No, not at all,' Tilda soothed, because she was pleased to learn that Rashad had considered her of sufficient importance in his life to have told his family about her. At the same time, though, it made her even more determined to find out what had so totally destroyed his faith in her. Had he seen her with a work colleague or another student that summer? Misinterpreted what he had seen? Did he have a problem with jealousy? Had someone lied about her?

A diversion was created by the arrival of a brass-bound wooden box inlaid with mother-of-pearl. Tilda eased up the lid and displayed, to a chorus of 'oohs' and 'aahs,' an intricate head-dress of beaten golden coins and an incredible quantity of ornate turquoise jewellery. Evidently last worn by Rashad's mother on the occasion of her marriage, the antique necklaces, earrings and bracelets had been passed down through many generations of brides.

Tilda sat while her hair was styled and her make-up done. Her sisters' steadily widening eyes warned her that the end result was likely to be very different from what she was accustomed to. A wonderfully colourful hand-embroidered and beaded kaftan was extended for her admiration. Only when she was finally dressed was she allowed to see herself in the mirror.

'Welcome to the sixteenth century!' Katie whispered cheekily in Tilda's ear.

From her kohl-lined, glittering turquoise-shadowed eyes to the silvery fairness of her hair, which fell like a gleaming sheet of silk below the bridal headdress, there was a dazzling barbaric splendour to her appearance. Tilda wondered if Rashad would go for the traditional Bakhari bride look and she rather thought he would.

She was led into a huge richly decorated room filled with people, but the only person she was truly aware of was Rashad. He wore an army dress uniform in royal-blue and gold, a sword hanging by his side. Her heart skipped a beat as soon as she saw him. She let the inner wall of her pride soften for an instant and admitted to herself that she didn't just find Rashad madly, insanely sexy and attractive. That was only a part of what drew her to him. The truth was that she had never got over the secret conviction that he was the love of her life. Although he had hurt and disappointed her, he had still awakened feelings stronger than any other man could hope to match. She still loved him. Perhaps, she reasoned ruefully, now that they were husband and wife, it really was time that she stopped fighting with him and gave him a second chance.

On cue, Rashad gripped her hand and murmured with flatteringly impressed conviction. 'You look so beautiful—it is wrong of me to think it, but every man here must envy me.'

Delighted that she had been correct in assuming that the medieval theme would be a winning success, Tilda drifted dreamily through the ceremony that followed. Her heart open to her emotions and her love acknowledged, she felt curiously at peace with herself. The reception started with a lavish feast. She sat by Rashad's side in their carved thronelike chairs and, with a calm smile on her lips, watched a ceremonial display of dancing with swords, whips and bloodthirsty shouts. After the folk dances came poetry readings and songs and the presentation of magnificent gifts. They went out onto a balcony to watch a camel race taking place beyond the walls.

In the noisy debate that took place at the end of the race, Rashad closed a hand over hers and tugged her back indoors and down a quiet staircase. 'Now at last we can be alone.'

'We can just vanish in the middle of it all?'

Rashad surveyed her with scorching golden eyes and brought his hungry mouth down on hers with passionate force. As an answer it was very effective. Her consciousness of the world around her went into a crazy tail-spin until he lifted his imperious dark head again.

'You've spent virtually the whole of the last month ignoring me!' Tilda recovered enough to splutter.

'But you made it plain that you wanted to be left alone,' Rashad reminded her darkly, walking her down the stairs at a pace she could manage in her long dress and high heels. 'You said you wanted to sleep apart from me.'

As Tilda paused to look up at him a sensual frisson of awareness slivered through her body. 'Not tonight, *but*—'

'No conditions,' Rashad slotted in.

'Just one tiny one,' Tilda told him winsomely, noting the way his devouring gaze was glued to her and feeling an intoxicating sense of her feminine power. 'You have to tell me what really happened five years ago. I want to know what made you turn against me.'

Seriously disconcerted by that demand, Rashad breathed, 'You want to rake up the past on our wedding night? Are you crazy?'

'Don't I have a right to know?'

'Yes,' he conceded, but with a reluctance she could feel, 'but not tonight.'

Tilda supposed he had a point and his admission that she had a right to know mollified her a little. Even so, she did not want to drop the subject until she had received an answer that she could depend on. 'What sort of evidence do you have?'

'A security file,' Rashad divulged, in the hope that revealing the source of his knowledge would persuade her into a diplomatic retreat. He could see no point in putting either of them through the discomfort of examining evidence that she would only find degrading.

Tilda was taken aback by that admission. 'And how the heck did you get hold of a security file?'

'It's been in my possession for a while. No one else has seen it,' he grated tightly. 'Right now it's in my briefcase.'

Satisfied by that admission, if a little spooked by the strength of his reaction, Tilda said nothing more; he'd listened to her request and acted on it. Tomorrow or the next day would be soon enough to resurrect the past. For the present, Tilda realised that she was more interested in making the most of her wedding day.

CHAPTER NINE

THE magnificent main bedroom suite, which neither Rashad nor Tilda had occupied before, was bedecked with flowers and bore more than a passing resemblance to a fairy-tale bower. Tilda was enchanted.

Rashad watched her reverently touch a snowy-white lily blossom. He moved forward to grasp her hand gently in his. 'This is my wedding gift to you.' He threaded a stunning oval diamond ring onto her finger. 'A betrothal ring. We were never engaged but I would like this ring to signify a new beginning for us.'

Her eyes prickled. The diamonds glittered with breathtaking brilliance. She was very touched by what he had just said, because he was offering her heart's desire. More than anything else she wanted to believe that she had a proper future with him. His choice of gift told her so much more than he would have managed to say. 'It's absolutely gorgeous.'

Rashad detached the coin headdress from her hair with great care and set it aside. Beautiful dark eyes serious below his luxuriant black lashes, he removed the turquoise jewellery piece by piece. 'It meant much to me to see you wear these gems.'

'Did anyone ever tell you how amazing you look in army uniform?' Tilda muttered helplessly.

'No,' Rashad said truthfully, and an amused smile lightened his solemn expression.

'Well, you do,' she told him gruffly.

'I want you so much I hurt,' Rashad breathed not quite steadily, letting the tip of his tongue delve between her readily parted lips.

As he leant closer she felt the hard evidence of his arousal through his clothing and a combination of nerves and excitement gripped her. He detached his sword belt and undid his jacket. She tugged it off him with hands that were clumsy with impatience. She had waited too long for him. She wondered if he would realise that he was her first lover. She hoped so. Then he would have to accept how wrong he had been about her and she supposed she would graciously accept his heartfelt apologies.

He undid the tight sash at her waist and unzipped the ornate and heavy kaftan, easing the rich fabric down slowly over her hips. Desire sparked low in her pelvis and she pressed her slim thighs together in embarrassment. Tiny little tremors were running through her slender figure. She stretched up and found his wide, sexy mouth again for herself. He held her there entrapped, one lean hand braced to her spine, the ripe swell of her breasts crushed by the powerful wall of his chest. As he captured her lips with shattering urgency her heart thumped an upbeat tempo inside her ribcage and a delicious surge of heat warmed her belly. His tongue plundered the soft recesses of her mouth, teaching her a wickedly erotic rhythm that made her whimper low in her throat with surprise and pleasure.

Golden eyes smouldering like the heart of a fire, Rashad set her back from him and removed the gossamer fine silk slip she wore. 'So many unnecessary layers,' he complained thickly.

Still clad in bra and briefs, Tilda reddened, wildly conscious of his appraisal as he shed his uniform. Watching in guilty fascination, she thought how beautiful he was from the smooth golden skin of his wide, sculpted shoulders to the hard, muscular breadth of his chest and his long, lean, hair-roughened thighs. Her admiring scrutiny jolted to a sudden halt just below the low-slung waistband of his boxers, where the explicit outline of his bold maleness was all too obvious to her disconcerted eyes. Hastily she glanced away, a tiny frisson of mingled response and alarm gripping her.

'Come here,' he urged.

'Can we do this really slowly?' Tilda asked abruptly.

Surprise and amusement made Rashad smile. With quiet confidence he let his long brown fingers feather through her pale silky ringlets in a soothing motion. 'What are you scared of? Surely not of me?'

Tilda went pink, mortified that she had let herself down with that nervous and all-too-revealing question. 'Don't be daft.'

Unhooking her bra with deft assurance, Rashad vented a husky sound of satisfaction and lifted his hands to cup the full, firm mounds of creamy flesh that tumbled free. 'I promise that you will know only pleasure in this bed tonight.'

Tilda remained tense. 'I'm not as experienced as you seem to think.'

His stubborn jaw line tautened, for he did not want to think of anything that might awaken thoughts of the men with whom she had betrayed his trust. He shut out that statement and wiped the very memory of it from his mind. If he let anger touch him again he feared that his promise of a new beginning would become empty, meaningless words and so he made no answer. Instead, he bent his head to kiss her into silence again and he stroked the delicate coral pink buds that crowned her breasts with skilful fingers.

The liquid sensation at the juncture of Tilda's thighs became a knot of almost painful anticipation. She sucked in an audible breath, but a gasp of disconcertion was wrenched from her when he pulled her down across his thighs, though she had no thought of protest. He used his tongue to lash a lush, pouting nipple with wicked expertise. He followed that bold caress with the gliding graze of his teeth, tormenting the tender peaks into rigid, straining points.

'Rashad…' she gasped, her hips squirming in a forlorn attempt to assuage the throb of need he had awakened.

'You like that?' Venting a soft laugh of satisfaction, Rashad framed her face with lean brown fingers to hold her still. 'I think you will like everything I do.'

He tasted her swollen mouth with erotic urgency and eased a hand beneath her hips to remove her last garment. Suddenly aware that she was totally naked, Tilda tensed and there was a hint of insecurity in the way her tongue twinned with his. Rising with her in his strong arms, he tumbled her gently down amongst the pillows. Removing his boxer shorts, he joined her on the bed. His rawly appreciative gaze feasted on the pale rounded contours of her shapely body. She lay there, her entire skin surface buzzing with a wanton response that not even an attack of almost paralysing shyness could kill.

'I want to please you,' Rashad muttered huskily. 'Just as you will wish to please me.'

'Please you?' she whispered uncertainly.

He took her hand and closed her fingers round that part of him that she had rigorously avoided looking at. The size of him dismayed her, even while the offer of such blatant intimacy fascinated her. Her face flamed at the iron-hard heat and satin smoothness of his rigid shaft. Uncertain though she was, curiosity took over. When he rested back against the pillows and groaned with uninhibited pleasure, answering heat slivered through her and centred on the damp, tender heart of her.

'How am I doing?' Tilda whispered shakily

'Too well for my control.' Rashad laced possessive fingers in her hair and devoured her luscious mouth in an almost punitive kiss while he spread her back against the pillows. He skimmed teasing fingers through the pale blond curls below her belly and she shivered, madly, wantonly aware of the hot, moist heat of that hidden place. He found the tenderest spot of all and she moaned and pushed her flushed face into his shoulder, alternately taut and melting with delight in response. She was wildly sensitive to his erotic skill. Her head moved restively back and forth, her spine incurving in a helpless attempt to release the unbearable tension rising inside her. He tested the slick, wet heat of her with a single finger. Consumed by the sheer force of her own response, she cried out, her senses scattered with need.

She had never dreamt that she could want and crave as she did at that moment. 'Rashad... please!'

But only when the ache for fulfilment had become a torment did he angle her back, sliding lithely and surely between her thighs. She was frantic by that stage, urging him on with eager, clutching fingers. With an earthy sound of male pleasure he eased a path into her delicate passage, restraining himself with difficulty as she was very tight.

'You feel marvellous,' he breathed raggedly.

Tilda was past speech, all her needs pent up in the violence of the hunger he had aroused and the astonishing newness of what he was making her feel. Only when he deepened his penetration did she feel discomfort. It took her entirely by surprise and was swiftly followed by a sharp stab of pain as he completed his possession. That final pang wrung an involuntary cry from her lips.

'Tilda...' In bewilderment, Rashad angled back from her and stared down at her. For a split second he had thought he felt a barrier, but he could not bring himself to voice what he believed would be a foolish question. Of course she could not have been a virgin. Of course it must have been his imagination. 'Have I hurt you?'

'No...no,' she mumbled, scarcely knowing what she was saying for she was not in the mood for a post-mortem. All momentary discomfort now forgotten, her body was tingling and aching with desire. She was on the thrilling edge of a sensual precipice, her excitement eager and ready to fly high again. That quickening sensation of overwhelming need made her feverishly impatient and she arched up to him in a wholly instinctive movement of encouragement.

With a roughened groan, Rashad succumbed to her provocative invitation and embedded himself again in the sweet oblivion of her body. The hot, virile glide of his flesh within hers submerged her in a sensual world of the purest pleasure. Enthralled by the discovery, she rose up to him and he thrust again. The potent masculine rhythm that he set increased her hunger for him, banishing all awareness of everything but the excitement he had unleashed. At a delirious peak of ravenous need, she reached a glorious climax and abandoned herself to the sweet convulsions of writhing pleasure that engulfed her.

Afterwards, enveloped in a heavy languor, she wondered abstractedly if she would ever move again. Inside she felt like warm, melting honey and buoyantly happy. She was amazed by how close she now felt to Rashad. He kissed her slow and deep and then rolled over, carrying her with him. Content to be held, she snuggled into him, revelling in the achingly familiar scent of his skin. Beneath her cheek, his heart had a steady, reassuring beat.

With a rueful sigh, Rashad eased her up level with him and subjected her to the onslaught of frowning dark golden eyes. 'I hurt you...I'm sorry.'

'You noticed, didn't you? But you are so stubborn,' Tilda murmured rather tenderly, running a slim forefinger along the taut line of his passionate mouth. 'So stubborn that you won't put two and two together and come up with the right answer. Well, it seems that I'll have to do it for you. I was a virgin.'

Rashad frowned down at her in disbelief. 'That's not possible,' he muttered half under his breath.

Tilda pulled herself up against the pillows and winced at the unexpected pang of tenderness that reminded her of how intimately entwined they had been just minutes earlier.

In an equally sudden movement, Rashad sat up, dislodging the bedding. He went very still when he saw the evidence of her lost innocence on the white sheet. He was so stunned to appreciate that he had not been mistaken in his suspicions that he was silenced. There could have been no other men in her life, not even *one* other man, or even a single serious affair. It should have been impossible but he looked down into her clear, expectant eyes and knew it was not, for there was fearlessness in that look that challenged him to disbelieve her again.

'So now you have to explain yourself…and a little humility would go a long way,' Tilda told him gently, positively basking in a sense of power and willing to offer helpful hints. 'Are you just a paranoiacally jealous guy? Because I really do need to know, if that's the problem.'

'That's not the problem,' Rashad breathed stiltedly.

'I want to see that file—'

'That is impossible.' Rashad could now imagine nothing more disastrous than to show her the sleazy file that had destroyed his faith in her. What an insult that would be to add to the original injury!

'You don't have a choice.'

'I have wronged you. I have misjudged you.' His head was pounding, he could barely think straight. He was fighting to absorb and contain the shock of what he had just found out. But he could not yet move beyond it because the fallout from that misjudgement five years back had been too great. 'I can only ask for your forgiveness.'

Tilda was seriously dissatisfied with that wooden response. She did not know exactly what she had expected from him but an ongoing refusal to do as she asked was not acceptable. 'The file?'

'No. I'm sorry.' In one strong movement, Rashad sprang out of bed, determined to get his head straight before he risked saying one more word to her. But, really, all he was conscious of was an enormous surge of bitterness and shame. 'I need a shower.'

In angry stupefaction, Tilda watched as his long, powerful golden back view vanished into the *en suite* bathroom. It didn't really matter to him, she thought painfully. She felt so horribly rejected. It didn't really matter that he had been her first lover, after all. Had she honestly believed that he would think that she was somehow more special? Wasn't that pathetic of her? All her hurt and anger turning destructively inward, she slid off the bed. What a fool she had made of herself! Why was she always doing that with him? She loved him, he lusted after her. Nothing had changed in five years. She was still looking for what she couldn't have, still hoping to somehow win what he didn't have to give her!

Despising her nakedness, she snatched up the wedding kaftan and wriggled her way into it, twisting round to do up the zip with frantic hands. She angled a shamed glance back at the tumbled bed, seeing it as the scene of her humiliation. Why had she thought a wedding ring would change anything? But why, most of all, had she allowed herself to believe that sexual intimacy would somehow make everything all right between them? She was on the way back to her own room when she recalled his grudging admission that the file he had mentioned was in his briefcase. Her eyes flashed. Without hesitation, she changed direction and headed for his office suite.

In the tiled wet room, Rashad stood with clenched fists under the powerful flow of the water. What did he say to her? Where were the words that could express his regret for his lack of trust? He was convinced that there were no words adequate to such a massive challenge. Especially after what he had gone on to do to Tilda and her family. He could blame only himself for the fact that he had added the pursuit of revenge to his tally of sins. Shame cut through him as keenly as the slash of a knife. He forced his taut shoulders back against the cold tiles. A boiling knot of rage was forming in place of his usual reasoned restraint. He shuddered at the memory of that file and what it had cost her… and him.

Such slander could only have been authorised at the very highest level. Sweat broke on Rashad's brow. He looked back five years. He remembered his father's lukewarm attitude to the prospect of his son taking an English wife. The king had urged his son to wait and consider before embarking on such an important commitment. Accustomed to independent, decisive action, Rashad had resented the suggestion that he could not be trusted to choose his own wife. No comment had been made when Rashad had let it be known that the relationship was at an end. Now Rashad was suspicious of what he had regarded at the time as his father's tactful silence. All his life he had awarded absolute loyalty to his parent. But he also knew that if the older man had sanctioned the sordid destruction of Tilda's reputation, he would never be able to forgive him for it. It was an issue, he recognised bleakly, that had to be dealt with immediately.

Rifling through Rashad's briefcase, Tilda finally came on what she sought. Swallowing hard, she withdrew the slim folder. She pushed the case back under the desk and returned to her bedroom, wondering if Rashad had noticed yet that she was missing and, if he had, what he would do about it. In the distance she could hear the sound of lively music and revelry: the royal wedding guests were still celebrating.

She sat down on the bed and opened the file. Her heart was in her mouth and she scolded herself, for all she was expecting to see was the source of the misunderstanding that she believed must have taken place—possibly, the name of a male friend had been erroneously linked with hers. Her address was given as the student house in which she had rented a room that summer. What she was not prepared to see was a fabrication of lies that listed a string of men, whom she had never heard of, and declared that they had all stayed overnight in her room. It was very precise as regards dates and times. Evidently she had been the victim of a sordid character assassination. She was devastated by the realisation that Rashad could have believed her capable of such rampant promiscuity.

Just as suddenly she was flooded with an explosive mix of rage and pain. When was enough enough? What did it say about her that she was willing to take whatever Rashad threw at her? Five years ago his rejection had destroyed her pride, her peace of mind and her happiness. Having encouraged her to care about him, he had broken her heart in the cruellest way available to him. When she had approached him recently in search of some compassion, he hadn't had a scrap of pity to spare. He had treated her like the dirt beneath his royal feet! He had offered her the chance to pay off the debts with her body. Only her concern for her family's future had persuaded her to agree to those degrading terms.

Yet when Rashad's ruthless plans had run aground and blown up in his face and he had needed *her* support, had she refused? Oh, no, she hadn't refused him anything but immediate sexual gratification! How could she have been so understanding? So ready to make allowances and forgive? In a passion of denial and self-loathing, she peeled off the kaftan and stalked through to the bathroom to wash her face clean of make-up. In the dressing room she dragged out fresh underwear, a shirt and cotton trousers, choosing from her own clothes, not from the designer wardrobe he had bought her. She was leaving him, she was going home to her mum. He could get stuffed! He could keep the fancy togs and all the ancestral jewellery, as well. She set the diamond engagement ring on the chest by the bed. She wasn't hanging on to that as though it were a sentimental keepsake! Her throat was thick with tears. It was better to travel light.

Tying her hair back, she put on a jacket and checked her passport. She ripped a sheet of paper out of a notebook and put it on top of the file, which she left lying on the bed. She wrote: 'You don't deserve me. I'm never coming back. I want a divorce.'

Only when she reached a side entrance of the palace did she appreciate that her bodyguards had seemingly come out of nowhere to follow her every step of the way. Consternation assailed her, because, not only had she hoped to make a sneaky exit, but she had also thought that she was barely recognisable in her plain and ordinary outfit.

'You would like a car, Your Royal Highness?' Musraf, the only English speaker in her protection team, asked with a low bow.

'Yes, thank you. I'm going to the airport.' Tilda endeavoured to behave as though a late run to the airport on her wedding night was perfectly normal. But the *Royal Highness* appellation almost totally unnerved her, because she had not known she was entitled to that label and it made anonymity seem even more of a forlorn hope.

Within minutes a limousine pulled up. Ushering her into it, Musraf enquired about the time of her flight.

'I want to go to London—but I haven't organised it yet,' Tilda informed him loftily.

She was assured that all such arrangements would be made for her. A private room was made available to her the instant she arrived at the airport. There she sat for two hours before being taken out to a private jet with the colours of the royal household painted on the tail fin. She crept aboard, feeling it was rather cheeky to leave Rashad by fleeing the country in one of his own aircraft. As it occurred to her that a wife who vanished within hours of a state wedding would cause him rather more serious embarrassment than that, she came up with an invented cover story for Musraf to relay to Rashad.

'Say my mother's not well and that's why I left in a hurry,' she instructed him helpfully before take-off.

Dawn was breaking when the jet landed in the U.K. Tilda had slept several hours and felt physically refreshed, but her spirits were at rock-bottom. Her protection team stayed close and while she was struggling to work out how to dismiss them politely her mobile phone rang.

'It's Rashad,' her husband murmured, making her stiffen in dismay. 'I'll see you at the town house in an hour.'

'Are you saying that you're in London, too?' Tilda vented in a hastily lowered voice that was the discreet version of a shriek. 'That's impossible!'

'One hour—'

'I'm going to see Mum—'

'One hour,' Rashad decreed.

'I won't be—'

'If you're not there I will come to Oxford for you,' Rashad informed her with ruthless clarity. 'You are my wife.'

Her face burning, Tilda thrust the phone back in her bag. He must have flown out of Bakhar very shortly after she had. His wife? His accidental wife would have been a more accurate description. How many women got married without even getting a proposal? Her teeth gritted. Well, if Rashad was that determined to stage a confrontation, he could have one with bells on! She had done nothing to be ashamed of. Although dating him in the first place struck her as being a hanging offence; he'd looked like trouble with a capital *T.* From start to finish, that was what he'd proved to be.

But even as she fought in self-defence to keep her furious defiance at a high, she remained miserably conscious of how devastating she had found the contents of that file. Actually seeing in print the kind of stuff that Rashad had believed her capable of had ripped any sentimental scales from her eyes. Love was a total waste of time with a guy who could happily make love to a woman he believed to be a total slut. That file had also resurrected the terrible pain that he had inflicted on her five years earlier. Well, there would be no more of it. He had done enough damage.

It was closer to two hours before Rashad strode into the drawing room of the town house where, just six weeks earlier, he had enforced his terms for their relationship. From the window, Tilda had watched him arrive and her chest had tightened and her breathing had shortened as though she was on the brink of a panic attack. She didn't want to notice that he looked drop-dead gorgeous in a very snazzy black designer suit. She didn't want to feel a hot, quivery sensation of near dizziness when she inadvertently collided with his smouldering tawny gaze.

Dark vibrations of anger were rippling through Rashad. 'You went into my briefcase to see that file.'

Her chin came up. 'I'd have blown up a safe to get a look at that file and I'm really glad I did.'

'That's not and will never be an excuse to walk out on our marriage.'

'I didn't walk, Rashad. I ran! And where were you? What was your reaction to the discovery that everything you accused me of, everything you dared to think about me, was hopelessly wrong?' Tilda demanded grittily, her wide eyes burning with tears. 'You went for a shower.'

Rashad vented a phrase in Arabic that sounded like a curse. 'I was in shock—I was upset—'

'Since when did you do "upset"?' Tilda threw at him bitterly. 'I've seen you cold, angry, scornful, silent. I've never seen you shocked or upset. Heaven forbid that anyone might suspect you have any real emotions!'

Rising to that challenge, Rashad settled blazing golden eyes on her. 'I was schooled from an early age not to reveal what I thought or I felt. Initially, that training was aimed at ensuring I had good manners, but before I was much older my safety and that of others often depended on my ability to stay in control. I have never had the freedom to parade my emotions as you do.'

Reminded of his background, Tilda squirmed and felt guilty, but she could not help feeling that her hurt was increased by the extent of his rigid self-discipline.

'Of course I was upset,' Rashad added in fierce continuance. 'How could you doubt it? The filthy lies in that file destroyed what we had found together five years ago.'

Her lashes lifted on mutinous turquoise eyes. 'No, *you* did that. You believed those filthy lies. You didn't give me a chance, not one single chance to speak up in my own defence.'

Rashad spread lean golden hands in a sudden driven movement that betrayed the level of his stress. 'I believed the source of that file to be above reproach. When I realised last night that the contents were an unforgivable tissue of lies designed to destroy our relationship, I had to know *who* was responsible. For that reason I approached my father first to find out if he had ordered the fabrication of that file.'

'Your *father?*' she echoed in surprise.

His lean, strong face was set in grim, angular lines. 'He was most distressed when I showed it to him. He had never seen it before.'

Fabrication or not, Tilda was aghast at him having showed that file to King Hazar. 'You actually showed the file to him?'

Rashad expelled his breath in a taut hiss. 'I wanted him to see for himself how you were maligned. He was appalled because he believes that he was indirectly responsible. He was concerned when I told him five years ago that I wanted to marry you.'

'You wanted to marry me way back then?' Tilda whispered in utter astonishment at that declaration.

'Let me explain this without interruptions,' Rashad urged, strain marking the set of his stubborn jaw line. 'My father is a man who did not become a ruler until he was past middle age. When I met you, he was still new to the throne

and nervous of many things. A son and heir pro-
posing to marry a foreigner was a source of
worry to him.'

'Yes,' Tilda conceded rather numbly.

'He shared his anxiety with his closest adviser,
who was at the time in charge of Bakhar's secret
service. No course of action was discussed. My
father did not feel he could interfere. But when I
later told him that my relationship with you was
over, he did wonder if the adviser had taken independent action. But he chose not to question him
or mention the suspicion to me and both those
omissions have been on his conscience ever since.
He called in Jasim, who is now his closest aide.
Jasim worked for my father's advisor five years
ago. He was aware of the file and very troubled
by what was done,' Rashad related heavily.

'At least someone knows right from wrong,'
Tilda muttered.

'Jasim was silent for fear of losing his position.
His former employer is now dead. Jasim saw
you when you visited the embassy in London
last month and when you came to my house. He

244   THE DESERT SHEIKH'S CAPTIVE WIFE

believed that I had discovered the truth about the file and he informed my father that you and I appeared to be seeing each other again.'

'But nobody came clean and owned up about the file until it was too late to matter.' Tilda had gone from shock that Rashad had been hoping to marry her five years earlier to overwhelming bitterness that the happiness that they had had then had been cruelly stolen from them. 'And nobody's going to pay for what was done to me or my reputation, either.'

Rashad was watching her every move. 'Haven't we all paid many times over?'

A sharp little laugh was dragged from Tilda. She turned from him to stare sightlessly out of the window overlooking the handsome early Victorian city square. 'I don't think five years of consorting with gorgeous supermodels and actresses and socialites was that much of a penance for you, Rashad.'

Rashad turned an ashen shade below his bronzed skin. He was willing her to look at him and she would not. There was a distance in her that he had never seen before. He did not know what to say to her. He could not deny the super-models, or the actresses or the socialites, but not one of them had been blonde because it would have reminded him too much of her. Not one of them had brought him happiness. Not one of them had been her.

'I did not forget you. I was never able to forget,' he breathed flatly.

Tilda was unimpressed. 'Only because of the insult to your pride. That rankled with you. You wanted revenge.'

'I wanted you back—'

'You wanted revenge. As if it wasn't enough that you just dumped me without a word. As if it wasn't enough that I had to see you kissing another woman. As if it wasn't enough that you left my mother loaded with debt!' Tilda flung at him chokily, striving not to parade her emotions in the manner he had described.

In response to that hail of accusations, his tawny gaze remained bleak. 'What you say is true. I have no defence to offer.'

'But do you know what your biggest sin is? That you didn't care enough about me or what we had to confront me or even doubt that file!' Tilda condemned fiercely, raging resentment finally breaking through her hollow sense of bitterness. 'You put your pride first.'

'I wouldn't now,' Rashad murmured in a roughened undertone.

'Oh, yes, you would. Last night, instead of concentrating on me, you went for a blasted shower and then you went off to see your father! You wanted someone to blame. You couldn't put me or my feelings first even then,' she accused shakily.

'That is not how it was.' Rashad drew in a deep shuddering breath. 'I was so angry at what we had lost—'

'You didn't lose me; you dumped me!'

Lean, vibrantly handsome features taut over his superb bone structure, Rashad dealt her a resolute dark golden appraisal. 'I know how many mistakes I have made with you, but I won't give up trying. I refuse to accept that the past should be allowed to wreck our marriage.'

'But that marriage is less than I deserve and I'm not settling for it,' Tilda protested vehemently. 'Your father is also obviously dead set against even having me in the family, although he was too well mannered to reveal those reservations to me.'

'My father is not against you,' Rashad asserted with assurance. 'Did I not tell you how much he regretted his doubts when I first knew you? It seems that ever since he has been haunted by the fear that he was responsible for the end of our relationship. He is very pleased that we are married and most impressed by the way you have taken on a public role.'

Tilda shook her silvery fair head. 'But I'm only your wife now because your revenge rebounded on you. When I saw that file, I just felt sick with anger that you had believed that rubbish... I couldn't ever forgive you for that.'

'But you are still my wife and it would go against my very nature to let you leave me,' Rashad responded quietly. 'I will do everything within my power to keep you. My bad judgement caused this. I believe that I can make our marriage what you deserve.'

The tears that she refused to shed were strangling her. Her throat ached and she could barely swallow. He was blaming himself for everything and, contrary as she was, she didn't like that. She was conscious of how hard he worked in every corner of his life. He carried a huge load of responsibility. It seemed wrong that he should feel forced to work at his marriage, as well. It had been his father's weakness and reluctance to be honest with his son that had created the situation. Rashad had been set up for a fall just like her and he was a warrior, born and bred, and he had responded with natural aggression.

She hated the fact that she was already making excuses for him. She felt like someone hovering indecisively while the last lifeboat was lowered from a sinking ship. That sinking ship was her image of what it would be like for her to live in a loveless marriage. In such a union, she would never feel truly necessary or special to him and she would always be forced to keep the emotional stuff low-key for fear of making him feel uncomfortable. The very knowledge that she wasn't loved would only make her continually try harder to be the best possible wife, and the most she could ever hope for in return would be appreciation and acceptance.

Involuntarily, driven by forces stronger than her will-power, Tilda stole a glance at Rashad and it was as if her very body was screaming at the threat of having to survive without him. For once, that response had nothing to do with his dazzling sexual magnetism. He might as well have chained her to him, she acknowledged bitterly, for there was a deep abiding need within her to be with him and to grasp at whatever closeness he could offer. Even though deep down inside she was still seething with indignant pain and anger over that hateful file, she knew that she still loved him enough for both of them. Walking off into the sunset with her pride intact was only going to make her wretchedly unhappy.

In an effort to bolster her mood, Tilda reminded herself that she had seriously undervalued her importance to Rashad when he was a student. She had assumed that all he had ever been after was a good time—primarily a good time in bed—while instead he had been making plans to marry her. Energised by that tantalising information, she fixed glimmering turquoise eyes on him. 'Were you in love with me five years ago?'

Rashad froze. He looked like a guy confronted by a firing squad without warning. 'I…' A tiny muscle pulled taut at the edge of his wide, sensual, unsmiling mouth. 'I liked you very much.'

It was a response that would have delighted her had they both been aged around ten years old.

Recognising that he had said the wrong thing, Rashad said abruptly, 'If I say I loved you, will you stay with me?'

And that telling response from Rashad, who barely uttered a word without triple-checking it in moments of stress, shed blinding light on his motives for Tilda. Never had she felt more ashamed of herself. She had him over a barrel. Within twenty-four hours of the televised state wedding she had scarpered. Angry, hurt and humiliated and needing to hit back the only way she knew how, she had run away. Doubtless Rashad thought her behaviour had been very immature. He had had to follow her and try to persuade her to return to Bakhar with him. What choice did he have? If his wife abandoned him he, along with every Bakhari, would feel they had lost face because he had picked the wrong wife. It wasn't fair to ask him if he had loved her.

'I think we should have some breakfast. Have you eaten?' Tilda enquired woodenly in a change of subject aimed at politely and quickly burying her stupid question and his revealing response.

His winged ebony brows drew together. She could see him struggling to master his bewilderment. 'No. I could not eat.'

Tilda drew in an irregular breath. She trod over to the bell in the wall and pressed it. The silence swirled like a stormy sea full of dangerous depths. A manservant appeared and she ordered breakfast in slow, careful Arabic.

Shaken up by the question she had asked, Rashad had felt able to tell her anything she wanted to hear, even if it meant lying for the first time in his life. But he had only felt that way for about ten seconds, for free speech or lies struck him as extremely dangerous in the current climate. He knew exactly how he felt about her. She was his wife with all that encompassed and he wanted, quite naturally, to take her home again.

'You are learning quickly,' Rashad murmured a shade unevenly, stunning golden eyes screened by the thick black wedge of his lashes to a bright glimmer.

Tilda wondered whether he meant the language or how to kill stone-dead the sort of emotional scene that she knew he found excruciating. 'I think I'd like to take the opportunity to see my mother while we're here,' she informed him prosaically.

'An excellent idea.'

'Both of us should visit,' she added, in case he had not yet got the message she was trying to give.

'Of course.'

The silence rushed back round them again.

'So, are we having a honeymoon?' Tilda heard herself ask rather loudly in the hope that he would comprehend the meaning of that less-than-subtle query.

Rashad stayed very still and then a charismatic smile flashed across his beautiful mouth, all the strain there put to flight by that query. 'It was already planned. Why do you think I've been working so hard in recent weeks? I needed to free up some time.'

That smile made Tilda's heart flip and the inside of her mouth run dry. That smile had sufficient pulling power to make her run up a mountain. She wanted to race across the room and fling herself at him like an eager puppy. She thought it fortunate that just at that moment the announcement that breakfast awaited them prevented her from embarrassing him to that extent.

When Tilda and Rashad visited her mother's home later that day in what Tilda felt was a welcome distraction after all the drama, they found Evan Jerrold cosily enjoying afternoon tea and home-made scones. Beth was overjoyed by the arrival of her daughter and son-in-law and Evan quickly excused himself. But Rashad spoke to the older man at some length, while Tilda talked to her mother. She was very pleased when the older woman confided that Evan had persuaded her to walk out of the front door and sit in his car just a few feet away for a few minutes the previous day.

'And you managed to do that without having a panic attack?' Tilda was amazed, because all Beth's children had made repeated efforts to coax their mother into trying to fight her phobia rather than totally surrendering to it.

'Evan's so confident. It did take me nearly two weeks to work myself up to walking out the front door. But I have to learn how to manage now that you're married to Rashad. Aubrey will be leaving home soon, as well,' Beth pointed out. 'I need to be more independent.'

The older woman passed her daughter several letters that had come for her. While Beth made fresh tea, Tilda went through her post. The final envelope was addressed in unfamiliar handwriting. She tore it open and withdrew a sheet of paper. It bore a poor quality photocopied image of a blonde woman dancing in a cage. A pulse started beating very fast at the foot of Tilda's throat. She peered at it in horror. It could have been her, or just as easily it could've been someone else. It was impossible to tell. Below the image, a mobile phone number was printed.

'I've made more tea!' Beth called as Tilda ducked into the dining room to make a call in private.

'I'll only be a couple of minutes.' Tilda closed the door and rang the number.

She recognised Scott's voice the moment he answered. Her tummy gave a sick lurch and she snatched in a steadying breath. 'It's Tilda. Why did you send me that picture?'

'I've got some actual photos of you doing your little dance.'

Her fingers tightened round her mobile phone. 'I don't remember anyone taking photos that night. I don't believe you.'

'It's up to you what you want to believe. But now you're royalty, those photos must be worth a packet. I reckon Rashad would pay a tidy sum to keep them all to himself.' Her former stepfather loosed a seedy chuckle. 'Of course, if you're not interested, just say. A half-naked blond princess in a cage would go down a treat with the gutter press.'

Tilda felt sick. Scott Morrison was blackmailing her. Had someone taken photos of her? His creepy mate, Pete, perhaps? She had no idea. A half-naked blond princess in a cage would be a much bigger source of humiliation to Rashad and his family than a runaway wife. She cringed at the prospect of such pictures appearing in print. 'How much do you want for the photos?'

'I thought you'd see it my way and keep it in the family. I want fifty grand.'

Although she was as white as a sheet, Tilda decided to call his bluff. 'Then I'll have to go to Rashad for the money because I don't have access to that kind of cash.'

'Leave him out of it,' Scott hastened to tell her, his agitation at the suggestion that she involve

Rashad audible. 'Keeping you on a shoestring, is he? How much cash can you raise in a hurry?'

'Maybe five thousand,' she mumbled shame-facedly for she knew she was doing the wrong thing. Everyone knew it was stupid to give way to blackmail. She knew it, too, but just the idea of Rashad seeing a photo of her in that cage again made her feel physically ill. She was convinced it would mean the end of her marriage. She had not spent any of the allowance that Rashad had put in a bank account for her. She told herself that using Rashad's money to get the photos back was a lesser evil than embarrassing him with the pictorial proof of her teenaged mistake.

Scott argued volubly, and then finally said he'd accept the payment if that was the best she could offer.

The door opened and Tilda gave a nervous start. Rashad was framed in the doorway. He quirked a sleek dark brow that questioned her obvious tension.

'I'll send you a cheque,' Tilda told Scott gruffly and hurriedly finished the call.

'Is there something wrong?' Rashad enquired, beautiful dark golden eyes welded to her pale, anxious face.

'No, nothing…just a stupid bill I forgot about. Embarrassing,' she mumbled, her teeth near to chattering at the very thought of him finding out what she was planning to do.

'My staff will take care of it. Let me have the details,' Rashad instructed.

'No, I'll see to it myself. When are we flying back to Bakhar?'

'Only when you wish.'

Tilda studied his gold silk tie with fixed attention. She did not dare meet his gaze, for he was far too keen and clever an observer. After that nasty little chat with Scott, Bakhar somehow seemed to shine like a safe haven on a wonderfully distant horizon. 'Could we leave tonight?'

When Rashad spoke, his surprise at that request was patent in his dark deep drawl. 'I thought you might prefer somewhere more cosmopolitan for our honeymoon…Paris, Rio—'

'The Palace of the Lions. You never did get

around to showing me the harem,' Tilda reminded him, feeling that that remote desert location would be comfortingly out of reach of Scott and his machinations.

CHAPTER TEN

'GOOD heavens…you and your grandfather might have been identical twins!' Tilda studied the photo of the long-departed Sharaf in his ceremonial robes with fascination, because she could see from where Rashad had inherited his classic bone structure.

Rashad splayed a possessive hand to her stomach to angle her back into connection with his lithe, powerful body. 'My father says his father's genes skipped a generation and turned up in me. Although I would like to believe that the likeness is only skin-deep, I definitely didn't inherit my father's mild temperament.'

'Have you abducted any women?' Tilda teased a little unevenly, physical contact with his lean, masculine frame stirring her into immediate awareness. Her nipples were pinching into tingling tension beneath the light cotton dress she wore.

'No. But if you hadn't agreed to give our marriage another chance I would have abducted you.'

Her eyes rounded in disbelief. 'Are you serious?'

Above her head, Rashad was trying not to smile. Nothing would have persuaded him to let her go. He bent his handsome dark head and his even white teeth gently grazed the tiny pulse point just below one soft feminine ear lobe. She shivered helplessly, warmth pooling in the pit of her tummy.

'Are you?' she repeated less evenly.

'I told you I wouldn't let you go in London.'

Cooler air brushed her breasts as he undid her wrap and stripped it gently down over her arms. She stood naked and captivated in the circle of his arms. He explored the sensitive peaks of her pouting breasts with a carnal skill that left her vibrating with quivering response against him. 'We only got up an hour ago,' she whispered.

'It's hard work being my favourite concubine,' Rashad intoned thickly.

'Is it?' she contrived to ask jerkily as long fingers smoothed down over her stomach to flirt with the silvery fair curls at the apex of her thighs.

'And when you signed up for the long haul of being a wife, the working conditions got much tougher. I hope you know how to stand up for your rights because I intend to take full advantage of having you within reach twenty-four hours a day.'

A breathless giggle was her sole response to that assurance. The unpleasantness of that episode with Scott had shaken her up, but she had sent the cheque. Surely, since he'd got what he wanted, any photos he had would be returned to her at her mother's address? Anyway, she might only have spent a week at the Palace of the Lions with Rashad, but she was happy. They'd never had the luxury of so much time together, and the more they were with each other, the less they wanted to be apart. She could see their reflections twinned in the mirror on the antique wardrobe. Her pale blond hair was bright as a banner against the darkness of his, her breasts wantonly bare beneath his bronzed hands. She thought she looked shameless. Shameless and fulfilled. With a certain indolent look in his gorgeous dark eyes, a particular note in his deep drawl, he could make her literally weak with longing. Her heart was pounding and her legs were trembling. She was leaning back against him to stay upright, wildly, dizzily conscious of his every caress.

With an earthy groan of satisfaction, Rashad explored the lush damp heat at the heart of her body. Spinning her round, he curved his hands to the soft swell of her hips and hoisted her up onto the table behind her. Her lashes lifted, passion-glazed eyes flying wide with disconcertion on his lean, dark, intent face.

'You'll like it,' Rashad growled in persuasion.

Before she could react, he parted her soft mouth and probed its moist interior with an erotic thrust of his tongue in a move that was as provocative as it was effective. He opened her thighs and touched her in ways that left her alternately whimpering and breathless, barely able to contain the throbbing ache of hunger that possessed her. Only when he had pitched her to a tormented edge of need did he tilt her back and plunge into her. Raw excitement sent a wave of blinding pleasure splintering through Tilda, and then another and another, until she was sobbing with mindless delight.

It was quite some time afterwards before she found voice and reason again. She was lying in bed where Rashad had carried her. At the high point of ecstasy she thought she might have screamed. Her face burned and she kept her eyes closed because she wasn't quite ready to look him in the eye yet. Five years earlier it had been the very intensity of what he could make her feel that had put her so much on her guard with him. Letting go of those defences gave her a wonderful sense of freedom.

A long taunting forefinger skimmed lazily down her spine. 'You liked it a lot,' Rashad husked, flipping her over and kissing her until she finally opened her eyes. 'I liked it even more. You are as passionate as I, and I don't have to restrain myself with you.'

Tilda focused on his lean, strong face and brushed weak fingers along the sensual line of his beautiful masculine mouth. He was wild in bed and she was discovering that she really loved that lack of inhibition.

His winged dark brows pleated in dismay and he drew back from her in a sudden movement. 'I forgot to use a condom.'

'Oh...well.' Tilda gave a vague accepting twitch of a slim shoulder and immediately began picturing a miniature Rashad with serious dark eyes, or a tiny bustling version of Durra chattering at every step. Although conceiving so early in their marriage was not what she would have planned, she was conscious of a warm feeling of anticipation.

Rashad studied her tautly. 'I might have gotten you pregnant,' he extended as though she might not have worked out that risk for herself.

'Well, it wouldn't be the end of the world, would it?'

'You wouldn't mind?'

'No, if it's meant to be, it's meant to be. I like children.'

His lean, darkly handsome face relaxed. He pulled her into his arms. 'You're amazing, but I shouldn't think we have anything to worry about,' he told her. 'We've been here for a week. Would you like to go to Cannes for a while? I own a house there.'

With a drowsy smile, Tilda rested her head on his shoulder. 'If you like.'

'Do you like?'

'Hmm…' she whispered, her eyes drifting shut, because she had decided that she would like anywhere as long as he was there with her.

Four weeks later, their honeymoon, which had been extended twice, was almost over. They had enjoyed a lengthy sun-soaked stay at Rashad's gloriously secluded estate in the South of France. He'd had been called away on business the day before. He was due back today, and Tilda was packing her jewellery in preparation for their departure later on. She was mentally taking note of the fact that once again her breasts felt a little tender. Her period was also ten days late. She had no intention of saying anything to Rashad until she had seen a doctor, but she suspected that she might have fallen pregnant. In fact, she was quite excited at the idea that she might already be carrying their first child and just a little worried that Rashad would be rather less enthusiastic.

As Rashad was expected to father the next generation of royals, having a family would naturally have featured on their future agenda. But it was very early in their marriage for her to have conceived. Although she knew that Rashad would act as if it were the best news he had ever heard, even if he didn't really feel that way, she was afraid that he would secretly regard a pregnant wife as a much less attractive option.

Heaving a sigh, she studied herself in the mirror, striving to imagine how she would look with a bigger bosom, no waist and a large tummy. Being of a practical disposition, Tilda scolded herself for agonising over what could not be changed. He wasn't in love with her and she knew it would be silly to try and pretend that that didn't make a difference. Her looks and how active she could be in and out of bed had to be crucial factors in the continuing success of their relationship. There would be no more flying here, there and everywhere, whenever the fancy took them, and water-skiing or horse riding might be too taxing, as well. They both enjoyed such activities, but now she would have to take her exercise in moderation. Would he get bored with her then?

In an abstracted mood she studied the glittering brilliance of a diamond bracelet. Rashad's most recent gift, it was as stylish as her engagement ring. She had also acquired a necklace and earrings. He had given her some gorgeous pieces. He was wonderfully generous. It was as though nothing pleased him more than pleasing her. Reminding herself of that truth, she walked out to the shaded terrace and sat down on a comfortable seat.

Beautiful mature gardens ran down to the beach. The estate also had an extensive stable. Tilda had never learned to ride, but Rashad and his family were horse-mad. He had coaxed Tilda out of her nerves and up onto the back of a doe-eyed mare. Able to relax on a horse that had only one speed—plodding—she had gone riding on the beach with him every morning. Well, she had plodded and watched him galloping very glamorously through the surf. He was a keen amateur polo player and he looked amazingly sexy on a horse.

Most evenings they had eaten out, dining everywhere from the grand restaurants in Cannes to the terraces below the palm trees. His reserve was fading fast. He was talking to her a lot more, teasing her more easily, as well. Their relationship had changed since that ghastly business over the file had come out into the open. More and more she was seeing the guy who had stolen her heart five years earlier.

Occasional arguments disturbed the peace and were usually settled in bed. Rashad was very energetic, very passionate and very stubborn. He had a will of iron and a naturally forceful personality. He was always going to be bossy. He was always going to think he

270 THE DESERT SHEIKH'S CAPTIVE WIFE

knew best about most things. What was infu-
riating was how often he was right. She was
totally, absolutely in love with him, she acknowledged dizzily.

'Tilda?' Rashad strode out onto the terrace,
looking spectacularly handsome in a lightweight
beige suit. 'I've been looking everywhere for you.'

'I didn't know you were back. I was enjoying
the view.' Tilda registered that his lean bronzed
features were unusually grave.

'Would you come inside? We have to talk,'
Rashad told her.

Tilda got up slowly and smoothed down her
skirt with uncertain hands. She had a tight,
nervous feeling in her tummy. ESP was telling her
that something was wrong, seriously wrong. She
entered the room that Rashad used as an office.
He lounged back against the edge of the desk,
brilliant dark eyes resting reflectively on her.

'You know, for some reason, I feel like a mis-
behaving kid called into the headmaster's office,'
Tilda confided tightly.

'Take a seat,' Rashad murmured gently.

Tilda sat down, but her back stayed poker-straight, because she knew she was not imagining the tense atmosphere.

'I'm going to ask you something and I would like you to be honest. What is your opinion of me as a husband?'

Tilda blinked and then opened her eyes very wide. 'S-seriously?' she stammered.

'Seriously.'

'Why are you asking me?'

'Indulge me just this once.'

'Well…you're marvellous company, even tempered…and patient. Great in bed.' Her face burned as Rashad elevated a questioning aristocratic brow that suggested she was barking up the wrong tree with her comments. 'Generous, thoughtful, fair.'

'I sound like a saint and I am not. You must be more candid and mention my faults.'

'I didn't say you had any faults,' Tilda disclaimed instantly, feeling that she was being steadily backed into a corner for some reason that she had not yet contrived to comprehend.

'Apart from being too clever for your own good sometimes.'

Rashad lifted a sheet of paper from the desktop and held it up for her to see. Tilda blenched, for it was the same photocopied picture of a woman dancing in a cage that Scott had sent her before. 'Where did you get that from?'

'Your mother forwarded it with your post. There was nothing on the envelope that indicated that it might be confidential, and it was opened by one of my staff, who thought it was a party invitation.'

Tilda extended her hand for the page and read the words below. 'Next instalment due,' it said, alongside Scott's phone number and address.

'It's been dealt with,' Rashad informed her quietly.

But shock and apprehension had made Tilda feel light-headed and sick, and she startled him as much as she startled herself at that moment by bursting into floods of tears.

Astonished and dismayed, Rashad lifted her out of the seat with a groaned apology. He smoothed her hair back from her damp brow. 'I think this may qualify as a too-clever-for-my-own-good moment,' he breathed rawly. 'I didn't intend to upset you. That was the very last result I wanted.'

'What did you expect when you showed me that horrible picture?' Tilda gasped chokily as he passed her a tissue and she mopped up. 'I was hoping I'd never have to see it again!'

Rashad banded his arms round her. 'You wouldn't have had to see it, if you had come to me with the first demand.'

Tilda stiffened and finally dared to look up at him. 'How do you know about that?'

'I saw Scott last night. That's where I was yesterday. Naturally, the instant I saw that picture, I knew that it could only have been sent to you as a form of threat. I confronted Morrison. There *are* no photos in existence of you dancing that night at the club.'

'Are you certain of that?'

'Yes,' Rashad confirmed. 'If he had had a genuine photo of you, he would have copied that, instead of using a stranger's on a photocopy.'

Tilda flushed. 'I suppose I should have thought of that.'

'It was an amateur effort to extort money. He wasn't clever enough to use a computer to fake a photo of you. It has been a very distasteful experience for you nonetheless. What was the first letter like?'

'The same picture was used,' she admitted tautly.

'You received it when we visited your mother. That was Morrison you spoke to on the phone regarding the bill that required payment, wasn't it?'

She nodded uncomfortably.

Dark deep-set eyes very direct in gaze, Rashad spread lean, shapely hands in a very expressive movement. 'It shames me that you would not come to me for help and support with this matter.'

'And rake up that cage business again? I'd sooner have died!' Tilda told him with a feeling shudder. 'I suppose that you already know that I paid Scott five thousand pounds?'

'Yes, and there's no hope of retrieving it, either. He's spent it.' Rashad grimaced with distaste. 'He's a nasty specimen, but he would never have dared to trouble you, had you come to me with his attempt to blackmail you. He's scared of me.'

'There's no real photos of me dancing in that cage… you're *sure?*' Tilda prompted, because she was still concerned and could not quite accept as yet that the threat had been removed.

'Certain.'

'I feel such an idiot now for having paid up.' She sighed. 'But I was just so horrified at the idea of some horrible sleazy-looking photo appearing in the newspapers and embarrassing you.'

'Even if there had been a photo we would have lived it down. I am more wise and tolerant than I was when you first knew me,' Rashad said wryly. 'I'm not that easily embarrassed.'

Tilda was amazed at his attitude. 'Do you mean that?'

'Of course I do.'

'Good. Then it's about time that I told you that it was your friends who put me in that cage to dance. They paid the manager to get me into it because it was your birthday!'

Rashad was very much disconcerted by this revelation. Tilda quite enjoyed that turning of the tables. She told him that she had found out that Scott had been taking money from her mother for several years, and that Morrison had most likely been behind the appearance of the paparazzi at the airport that day. He looked grim but was convinced that her former stepfather would cause no further annoyance.

'In my eyes, a husband's most basic role is to protect his wife from harm,' Rashad shared tautly. 'Yet you could not trust me enough to tell me that Morrison was blackmailing you.'

'It wasn't that I didn't trust you. I felt so guilty about the cage episode.'

'You have no need to feel guilty. But perhaps you did not have enough faith in me because I have been too slow to tell you what you mean to me.' His lean strong face was taut. 'Five years ago, you were everything I had ever wanted in a woman. In an instant I fell deeply in love with you. That's all it took.'

Tilda stared up at him in unconcealed surprise.

'You were my dream, my prize after many disappointments. I had been alone a long time. But I knew you did not feel the same way as I did—'

'Rashad,' she broke in emotively.

'I believed that if you had felt as much for me as I did for you, that you would have slept with me.'

Tilda was shaken by that candid admission. 'That's just not true. I really loved you, but I thought there was no future in it. I mean, you were going to be a king some day and I didn't want to be hurt. I thought if I kept our relationship light that it wouldn't hurt so much when you went back to Bakhar.'

'I had no idea. Wasn't it obvious that I was serious about you?'

'No. I was also terrified you would get me pregnant,' she admitted in a rush. 'I had a thing about that then—Mum always seemed to fall pregnant so easily.'

Rashad cupped her face with unsteady hands. 'If only we had talked about the things that really matter, but I didn't know how to. I just expected you to *know* what was in my heart.'

'But I did really love you an awful lot,' Tilda told him unsteadily. 'When you dumped me, it felt like my world had ended.'

His lustrous dark eyes were suspiciously bright and he bowed his handsome head over hers with a husky groan. 'I adored you. I would have given up everything for you, even the throne, and I think my father knew it, which gave him more reason to fear your power over me.'

Tilda was so close to him she could barely breathe and it still wasn't close enough. He had adored her, too? He crushed her to him and she rejoiced in his emotion.

'In five years without you, I was never once happy again. I am ashamed to admit it, but even if you had been a gold-digger I think you would still be my wife because I love you so much.'

'How long have you been in love with me?'

'For five years I called it hatred. I never got over you,' Rashad confessed in a driven undertone.

'Don't you realise how much I still love you?' Rashad studied her with doubt in his candid gaze.

'But how could you?'

'You say sorry very nicely. You're great with blackmailers, too. You're very handsome. You make me happy. I suppose that's the most important thing of all. When I'm with you, I'm just so happy!'

'You love me?' His spellbinding smile was beginning to curve his lips.

Tilda stretched up and kissed him, and that was all the encouragement he needed to kiss her back—breathless.

'Oh, and I think I might be pregnant,' she shared in an afterthought, deciding that she would never keep anything from him again. 'And I'm pleased.'

Rashad laughed out loud and surveyed her with near reverence. 'I must be the luckiest man alive.'

Feeling very much like the luckiest woman, Tilda let her eyes drift dreamily shut as he carried her off to bed. She suspected that the end of their honeymoon would be postponed for yet another few days....

Almost three years later, Tilda watched Rashad hunker down to open welcoming arms to his son and daughter.

Sharaf was almost two, a solid little boy who was tall for his age with black hair and blue eyes. Pyjama-clad, the child hurled himself at his father with a shout of delight and immediately started chattering. Rashad tucked his son under one arm and murmured gentle encouragement to the baby crawling laboriously towards him. Bethany was nine months old. Blond and brown-eyed, she had her father's charismatic smile and her mother's temper. As the Persian rug beneath her rumpled and impeded her progress she burst into tears and threw herself flat to sob. Rashad scooped her up and soothed her with an ease that revealed how comfortable he was handling his children. The little girl clung like a limpet and patted his face, beaming at him with love and approval.

It was the weekend and Tilda and Rashad often spent weekends at the Palace of the Lions, where privacy was usually assured. Sharaf had proved such a delight to his parents that they had decided to have another baby as soon as possible after his birth. He was a delightful child, forward for his age and very active. Tilda had had two straightforward pregnancies and was planning on waiting awhile before contemplating a third.

Her mother had recently married Evan Jerrold and was living in much more comfortable circumstances. It had taken a year and professional help for Beth to overcome her agoraphobia. It had been a tough challenge for her, but she was now a regular visitor to Bakhar. Tilda had been delighted by Beth's remarriage, for she had always liked Evan and she no longer worried about her parent in the same way that she once had. Her brother, Aubrey, had qualified as a doctor and Katie was at university. Her younger siblings, Megan and James, were doing well at school. It was a source of great satisfaction to

Tilda that she was still able to see a lot of her family. She often visited London with Rashad.

The king was a regular visitor to their home in the Great Palace for he was very fond of children. Tilda had become very relaxed around the unassuming older man. She led a very busy but fulfilling life. She had supervised the renovation of the Palace of the Lions. She also realised how lucky she was to always have ready assistance with the children and she made the most of it. She had taken up painting again, although she had privately reached the conclusion that, although she enjoyed the pursuit she was possibly a more talented accountant than she would ever be an artist. Even so, Rashad, who could hardly draw a recognisable stick figure, was hugely impressed by her every artistic endeavour and embarrassingly quick to show her work off to visitors.

Tilda lifted Bethany from her husband's arms. Their baby daughter was yawning. 'She's sleepy.'

Rashad leant down and claimed his wife's luscious mouth with a brief but hungry insistence that made her dizzily aware of his potent masculinity. She went pink and thought about how much she had missed, for he had been in New York for a week. Sometimes Tilda and the children travelled with him, but it wasn't always practical. Together they put Sharaf and Bethany to bed. They enjoyed such quiet family moments. Rashad told his son a bedtime story while Tilda gave their daughter a drink and tucked her into her cot.

'At last,' Rashad groaned, tugging her into his arms in the privacy of their bedroom. 'I couldn't wait to get back to you tonight.'

'Hmm…' A blissful smile on her lips, Tilda leant into the heat of his big, powerful body. 'Did I ever tell you how happy you make me?'

'I can live with being told again.' Stroking her hair back from a delicate cheekbone with tender fingers, Rashad studied her with possessive intensity. 'But I couldn't live without you… I love you more every day….'